D0261300

Colin Dann was born in Richmond, Surrey. His interest in natural history was fostered by studying the local wildlife in Richmond Park, and wildlife success came at the age of ten, when he won a London Schools Essay Competition set by the RSPCA. His prize was a copy of *The Wind in the Willows*. For many years he worked for Collins, the publishers. It was during this period that his concern for conservation led him to write his first novel, *The Animals of Farthing Wood*, which won the Arts Council National Award for Children's Literature in 1980.

Colin has since published seven further books in his Farthing Wood/White Deer Park sequence: *In the Grip of Winter* (1981), *Fox's Feud* (1982), *The Fox Cub Bold* (1983), *The Siege of White Deer Park* (1985), *In the Path of the Storm* (1989), *Battle for the Park* (1992) and *Farthing Wood – The Adventure Begins* (1994). These stories were made into a highly successful animation series for the BBC. Other titles by him include *The Ram of Sweetriver* (1986), *The Beach Dogs* (1988), *Just Nuffin* (1989), *A Great Escape* (1990), *A Legacy of Ghosts* (1991) and the City Cats trilogy, *King of the Vagabonds* (1987), *The City Cats* (1991) and *Copycat* (1997).

Nobody's Dog

By the same author:

The Animals of Farthing Wood
In the Grip of Winter
Fox's Feud
The Fox Cub Bold
The Siege of White Deer Park
The Ram of Sweetriver
King of the Vagabonds
The Beach Dogs
Just Nuffin
In the Path of the Storm
A Great Escape
The City Cats
A Legacy of Ghosts
Battle for the Park
Farthing Wood – The Adventure Begins
Copycat

Colin Dann

NOBODY'S DOG

HUTCHINSON
London   Sydney   Auckland   Johannesburg

First published in 1999

3 5 7 9 10 8 6 4 2

© Text Colin Dann 1999

Colin Dann has asserted his right under the Copyright, Designs and
Patents Act, 1988, to be identified as the author of
this work.

First published in the United Kingdom in 1999 by
Hutchinson Children's Books
Random House UK Limited
20 Vauxhall Bridge Road, London SW1V 2SA

Random House Australia (Pty) Limited
20 Alfred Street, Milsons Point, Sydney
New South Wales 2061, Australia

Random House New Zealand Limited
18 Poland Road, Glenfield
Auckland 10, New Zealand

Random House South Africa (Pty) Limited
Endulini, 5A Jubilee Road, Parktown 2193, South Africa

Random House UK Limited Reg. No. 954009

A CIP catalogue record for this book
is available from the British Library

Papers used by Random House UK Ltd are
natural, recyclable products, made from wood grown
in sustainable forests.
The manufacturing processes conform to the environmental
regulations of the country of origin.

ISBN 0 09 1716900 0

Phototypeset by Intype London Ltd
Printed in Great Britain by
Biddles Ltd, Guildford and King's Lynn

For Clive and Linda

'Still looking for your owner?' The voice was quiet but friendly.

Digby, a young border collie, let his front paws drop to the ground. He had been balancing on his hind legs, straining to peer through the grille in the door of his pen. As usual there had been nothing to see in the corridor outside; no sign that his present misery was likely to end. He turned sadly and saw a lean and grizzled black greyhound watching him. The dog had entered Digby's pen through the sliding door from the rear passage, which was used by the staff of the Dogs' Home to bring food or cleaning materials into the various dogs' quarters.

'They must think we're compatible,' the greyhound said, referring to the open door. 'Most dogs are confined alone, except for exercise. My pen's next to yours,' he explained.

'Oh yes – I see,' Digby murmured. 'I don't know much about this place. I haven't been here long.'

'No. And that's why you're still spending most of your time gazing out for a glimpse of your master. But I don't know why you're here at all, a handsome youngster like you.'

Digby's ears pricked up. 'Perhaps ... perhaps it's a mistake?' he asked hopefully.

'Perhaps.' The greyhound didn't sound very optimistic.

Digby's morose expression returned. Then he asked, 'How do you know so much about me?'

'I only know what I see,' the greyhound replied. 'If

I get on the shelf in my pen and stretch up, I can see into yours. I've felt very sorry for you. It's always the same for new dogs. They all believe they'll soon be fetched away again, when they first come in.' He sat down on the bare concrete floor. 'And then, as time goes on . . .' The greyhound's voice tailed away and he looked meaningfully at Digby.

Digby swallowed hard. He dared not dwell on the unspoken suggestion. 'I'm glad you came to see me,' he muttered. 'I'm not used to being alone, you see. I had company. There were two of us: my brother Tam and me.'

'Oh?' The greyhound was puzzled. 'Then how did you become separated?'

'I don't know; I don't understand it,' Digby replied miserably. 'One of my owners brought me here – it was the eldest one; the one who seems in control. I thought he would come back for me. I've never been left anywhere this long before. My brother was still at home when we left.'

'So you've no idea what's happened to him?'

'None at all. I think about him all the time. We were always together.'

'That's too sad. Well, look – let's not make ourselves any more unhappy. My name's Bouncing Jet Streak of Fleetwood. What's yours?'

Digby gaped. 'Er – Digby,' he stammered. 'What did you say you were called?'

'Oh, it's my kennel name. Call me Streak and forget the rest.'

'Kennel name?'

'Yes. You know – my pedigree. You must have a pedigree? You're a perfect border collie.'

'Actually I'm not,' Digby said. 'My mother was. But I think a little of something else crept in from my father.'

'Oh well – first cross,' Streak summed up. 'Anyway, you and I are unusual here. Most of the inmates are mere mongrels. Brought in off the street.' He sounded rather dismissive. 'You'll have heard some of them, I dare say?'

Digby shuddered. 'That endless barking! It's horrible. Some of them sound so frantic. And scared. And who's that really strident one that keeps yelling, "I'm the boss! I'm number one!"?'

'A big hulk of a dog who's always exercised alone. I've seen him. He's a bully. I can't see he's got any chance of being housed.'

'Housed?' Digby seized on the word. 'You . . . you mean . . . ?'

'Let me explain,' Streak said importantly. He lay down on the floor. Digby went to the recess in the wall where he had his sleeping blanket. He settled himself on it, resting his head on his paws, and regarded Streak steadily. 'You won't stay here,' the greyhound continued. 'A good-looking fellow like you is in great demand. I've seen how the outsiders linger by your pen.'

'Outsiders?'

'The human visitors. They prefer young animals. More appealing. You'll soon be picked out. And you'll have a new home.'

'But I don't want a new home,' Digby whined. 'I want my old one.'

'I know,' Streak answered kindly. 'Digby, you must forget all that. If your master decided to bring you to this place, then it's not likely he wanted to keep you. I'm sorry,' he added, seeing the abject expression on Digby's face. 'It's best to know where you stand. This is a home for abandoned and starving animals. It sounds awful, doesn't it? Don't be too downhearted. It's better to live with an owner who comes here and chooses you than one who abandoned you. Cheer up! You've more chance than I have. I've been here ages.'

Digby forgot his own misery for a moment. 'What happened to you?' he muttered.

'Past my best,' Streak replied succinctly. 'I was a racer. A champion. I could outrun everybody. Oh, I was well looked after then. But I got injured and I couldn't run any more. The men had no more use for me. So they dumped me here. I didn't realize at first what was going on. But I've learnt a lot while I've been here and I've been able to piece it all together. So you see – your future's not as bleak as mine. Who would want to provide a home for a greyhound who can't run any more?' Streak looked mournful. He got up. 'There; now I'm feeling sorry for *myself*. That doesn't do any good.' His bony head lifted as he heard a clatter. 'Food wagon's coming,' he announced briskly. 'I'll go now. We'll talk again.'

'Yes. Yes, please,' Digby answered eagerly. He liked the quietly spoken animal and was sorry he had to leave. 'So I might have a new home?' he murmured to himself, trying to accustom himself to the notion. 'But what about Tam? Won't I ever see him again? I don't think I could bear that. I wonder if he ever thinks about me?'

A young woman arrived with food. Digby licked his lips as the pellets rattled into his food bowl. He hadn't entirely lost his appetite. He stepped nervously from his bed, wagging his tail politely. His flattened ears betrayed his uncertainty.

'You're still not sure of me, are you?' the girl said kindly. 'We'll get used to each other, never fear. We're all dog-lovers here. And you're a fine boy, aren't you?' Digby's tail wagged more vigorously. He was indeed in the pink of health. His soft black and white coat gleamed. His nose glistened. His brown eyes were clear and intelligent. He was alert but jumpy; any sudden noise could make him flinch or flee according to its intensity. The girl gave him a gentle pat. Digby winced without meaning to. His tail dangled. 'Well, you're going to win someone's heart,' the girl remarked. She bustled about. Digby waited for her to leave before he approached his food.

Other dogs were barking in their eagerness to be fed, to be noticed by the girl on her rounds. The ones on the other side of the block had to wait longest. Some of them, consumed by frustration, made the building ring with their cries. Digby cringed and wolfed his food, ready to dart away at the slightest provocation.

'Poor things,' he whispered after swallowing his last gulp. 'This is a frightening place.'

When the block quietened he went automatically to the grille and peered out. Despite Streak's words he was unable to accept that he would never see his home or his human family again. The dull ache that had been with him since his abandonment flared up again. Why had he been brought here? What had he done? Even the walk to this place had been fun, as all walks were, except for the traffic noise along the main road. He hated that. But his master had shown no displeasure at his nervousness, no anger. Digby knew that his highly strung nature sometimes led to a loss of patience on the humans' side. But he'd never been punished for it. He had always felt the family made allowances for him, even though Tam, by comparison, seemed so calm and unflustered. And it had ended so horribly suddenly, his relationship with the family. The day of abandonment had shown no sign of being any different from any other. There had been no forewarning that anything was wrong. Right up to the moment when he and his master had entered this strange place, Digby had believed that he was simply on an outing. Once inside, however, he had known something was amiss. The appearance of the bleak compound, the tension in the air and the sharp scents of fear, hopelessness and anger, washed over the collie like the breaking of a dull wave. At once he was engulfed and, before he had any chance to make sense of it, his master was gone and a stranger was leading him deeper into the interior.

Since then an ache of longing and a kind of numbness had held him in their grip. He had paid no attention to the human visitors. What good to him were their faces, their voices, when all he wanted were those he had grown up with? Now, as he watched, people were entering the corridor in ones and twos. A man on his own came towards the collie and spoke to him. Digby dropped to his feet, disheartened. The voice was harsh-sounding and grating, about as unlike the ones he had been used to as was possible. Digby curled himself up on his blanket, shivering slightly and licking his chops repeatedly. 'I was loved,' he told himself. 'Surely I was. Wasn't I?' There was affection and – and – kindliness.' He thought of the daughter of the house. 'Millie was the best. She cared for me: I know it. Why did she let me come here?' Digby wanted to howl in his misery but he smothered the inclination. He knew it would bring a flurry of strangers to stare at him. So he lay quietly and tried to think about Tam. Finally he murmured, 'I hope Streak can visit me again.'

2

'I'm number one! I'm the boss! There's no one like me here! Look at me!' The big dog was bellowing again, trying to attract the attention of the visitors.

'Knock it off, will you?' another dog yapped. 'It's all we ever hear. Me, me, me! That's all you know.'

'Yes, belt up, will you, Number One?' snarled a third, using the big dog's nickname. 'Give us some peace.'

'Miserable runts, safe in your own pens!' roared Number One. 'You wouldn't dare face me in mine!' Exploding with frustration, the dog barked even louder, pausing only to race round and round the restricted space of his pen in a kind of frenzy.

Digby cowered on his blanket, disliking the coarse sounds, but so wrapped up in his own misfortune that he was unable to think for long about the other dogs' unhappiness. 'When will I get out of this?' he whispered to himself. 'Will Millie come to see me?' He let out a little whine. 'But she can't! She never goes out by herself. Oh!' He closed his eyes, trying in vain to blot out the noise. 'And what happens if *nobody* comes for you, like poor old Streak? Do you stay here for ever?' He started to howl, the prospect held such horror.

At once two or three other animals answered, howling their own fears into the void. There was a scrabbling at the wall adjoining Digby's pen. Streak had jumped on to his shelf and was peering down at his neighbour.

'Stop that!' he snapped. 'You'll put yourself in a panic.'

Digby looked up, his ears flat against his head. His

howling subsided. 'Streak,' he whispered hoarsely, 'what will happen to you?'

'Don't worry about me,' the greyhound answered. 'I'm an old hand here. I'll take what comes.'

His reply left Digby with a feeling of dissatisfaction. He had been hoping for some reassurance in case he ended up in the same plight.

'Just try to settle down,' Streak advised. 'Don't expect too much. You'll find it a lot easier. Time passes and then, one day – bingo! It'll all be over.'

'What will?'

'Your incarceration.'

'What does that mean?'

'Oh, you know – being cooped up here.'

'But you can't be sure, can you?' Digby persisted. 'Does every dog here find a home?'

Streak changed the subject. 'I'm coming round,' he said. 'I want to hear more about you and your brother. Perhaps I'll find a clue as to why you're here and he's not.'

It was quieter now. Number One had stopped barking. The food trolley had reached him. Streak came trotting into Digby's pen with his light, elastic steps. Warm spring sunlight bathed the enclosure from the windows above the rear passage. Digby sat up and watched Streak admiringly.

'No one would know you were injured,' he commented.

'I'm not any more,' Streak told him, waving his long thin tail in greeting. 'I sometimes dream I'm racing again. I can see the hare target ahead of me, always keeping its distance no matter how hard I run. I know I can't catch it and yet I try. I go faster. And faster. But it's always ahead of me, tantalizing me. Behind me comes the pack. I can hear their gasps as they try to match me. But they can no more catch up with me than I can catch that hare. I'm out on my own, my legs bunching and opening in flowing strides; bunching, opening again, eating up the ground. I feel I'm whirling, spinning round the track, round and round, every circuit swifter than the one before: head up, blood singing, tongue lolling—' Streak stopped abruptly.

'What's wrong?' Digby asked, enthralled. He wanted to hear more.

'Nothing. I always wake before the race ends. Every time the same. I know I'm going to win, then . . . phut! Something wakes me.'

'How wonderful to be able to run like that!' Digby had forgotten Streak had only been describing a dream.

The greyhound looked solemn. 'In reality it wasn't quite like that,' he said. 'In the end there were too many races. I was asked to do too much and that was how I got injured. And besides, as a racer, you don't have the same close bond with your owner as a pet dog does with his. It's a different sort of relationship. You're not a fireside companion. You're a working dog, really. Just like your breed in the country being kept to control sheep, I was kept to win races. That was my function.'

'Yes, I understand,' said Digby. 'I didn't have a function. Perhaps I'd have been better off if I had. I don't think border collies make ideal household pets.'

'Were you restless?'

'I'll say.'

'And your brother?'

'Tam has a calmer spirit. He didn't seem to mind those endless hours indoors.'

'Were you from the same litter?' Streak asked.

'Yes.'

'It's unusual for twins to have such different temperaments.'

'We're not that different,' said Digby. 'Tam simply doesn't get so agitated.'

'Tell me all about him.'

'Well,' said Digby, 'he was just always there. From my earliest memory right up until . . . until . . .'

'I know,' said Streak. 'Go on.'

'That's what's so awful,' Digby said miserably. 'He'll be wondering where I am. He must be. We were always together. I don't remember much about my mother. But Tam and I played together as puppies. We shared a basket, we went on walks with our owners, we were fed at the same time. He looks like me, except he has more black in his coat than I have. He used to laugh at me when I got nervous. He called it "going jangly".'

'When did you go "jangly"?'

'Whenever   something   unexpected   happened. Strange humans calling at the household, bangs or thuds inside or outside, thunder – oh, and when I had to walk near busy roads with all their roar and din. And I loathed it when my owners shouted at me or Tam or each other. How I detested being told off! I used to burrow under a chair or a table and skulk there for ages until tempers had cooled. Tam would come and give me a lick. He was good at comforting me. And so were the female humans.'

'I think I get the picture,' said Streak. 'You *are* a nervy one. Was your male owner cruel or frightening?'

'Never cruel. But he has a loud voice and he did lose patience with me quite often. I'm afraid I got so anxious about upsetting him that I became even more—'

'Jangly?' Streak interjected.

'Exactly. And I tried so hard to please him. Sometimes I succeeded. I know I did because he could also be warm and kind, and then it was wonderful and I felt so happy and relaxed and Tam and I thought we had the best home in the world.'

'But not always?'

'No. That was my fault. I couldn't check myself all the time. Millie, the young human, was very fond of me. Sometimes she and her father shouted at each other about me. I know it was about me because it used to happen after I'd been told off. It was ghastly.'

Streak looked at Digby steadily. 'Would you still choose to go back there?'

'Oh yes,' said Digby. 'I was loved there. And I loved them in return.'

A wistful look came into Streak's eyes. 'How wonderful,' he murmured.

Their conversation was interrupted by a sudden cry. A small dog was yapping excitedly, 'Bennie's going out! Bennie's going out!'

Streak pricked up his ears. Digby licked his lips and glanced at the greyhound for an explanation.

'That's Lily calling,' the older dog responded. 'Bennie's pen is next to hers. He must have been chosen.'

'By one of the outsiders?'

'Yes. This is how it happens. It's quite sudden. The visitors make a selection and you're taken away to another place to see how you like each other. Then, if all goes well, you're out of here and settling down with your new owners before you realize it. Some dogs come in here and go out again almost at once. But Bennie's been here a while.'

'Lucky dog,' said Digby. 'Just listen to Number One now! He sounds beside himself. Is it because he was overlooked again? It's so sad, all these unwanted animals shut up here together and none of us knowing why or when we're likely to leave.'

'It *is* sad,' Streak agreed. 'But there's no excuse for that racket. A lot of the dogs here have no manners at all.'

3

Under the greyhound's soothing influence Digby gradually managed to accept the regime of the Dogs' Home. He still ached for his old home, but in time he got used to the brisk, pleasant young staff who cared for the inmates. Streak was wonderful: always quiet and understanding. He never howled. His fatalistic approach set an example to Digby, who began to spend less time dwelling on his own unhappiness. Occasionally the occupants of the pens changed as a dog was chosen and another took its place. Otherwise each week was identical to the preceding one. Food, exercise, companionship, solitude, visitors, din. That was how the days were made up. Until a day came which was like no other.

For some time Digby had been taking a little more interest in the outsiders than he had at first. There were all kinds and all ages. Some had soft, inviting voices, others were boisterously friendly. Once in a while Digby would even show the faintest sign of friendliness back. A feeble wave of his tail or an appreciative look in response to some kind words was, however, as far as he ever permitted himself to go. And then, one afternoon, Frank arrived.

Frank was a tall, slim, dark-haired young man, dressed casually almost to the point of scruffiness in worn jeans and T-shirt and a leather jacket. He had an open, honest face which had the pink glow of someone who spent a lot of time in the fresh air. A small gold earring dangled from one ear. But it was his voice which Digby noticed first. The collie heard it drifting towards him along the corridor as Frank made his tour of the pens. Something about it made Digby curious. It was quite unlike any voice he had heard before. Many of the outsiders sounded sympathetic or compassionate. Frank did, too, but there was something else. There was a quality of understanding in his tone that was most unusual in a human, as though the young man had somehow experienced the same kind of suffering as the animals had; as though in some way he was on their level. As he came along the corridor all the dogs fell quiet – all those that were sensitive to his voice that is. Number One, of course, was barking so loudly he couldn't hear anything except himself. Digby trotted to the grille and stood on his hind legs. Frank was talking to Streak. Then he strolled up to Digby's pen. Man and dog held each other's gaze. Frank's brown eyes seemed to penetrate Digby's heart.

'Well, I wonder what you're doing in this place?' the young man said. 'I sometimes come in here to get out of the cold, and because I like to imagine I could have a dog of my own one day, but I bet you didn't choose to be here, did you? I wonder where you came from?' Digby seemed to understand every word. He whined and tried to lick the young man's hand. Frank smiled. His face glowed. 'It's as if we know each other,' he whispered. He lingered a while, talking softly, then murmured, 'How I wish I could take you with me,' and walked slowly on. Digby dropped back on all fours. A feeling of emptiness swept over him, unlike anything he had ever felt before. He stood motionless, his head hanging low. Number One was bellowing, 'Take *me*! Take *me*!' Digby didn't hear him.

For days he could think of nothing but the face and voice of the young man. Many other visitors came and went, showing varying degrees of interest in him, but Digby remembered none of them.

Then one day one of the young women who fed him entered his pen and slipped a leash round his neck. As he was led away, his ears barely registered Streak's plaintive voice calling, 'Farewell, Digby. Be happy – and make sure you don't come back.' He was brought to a room he hadn't seen before. There sat a middle-aged man wearing an anorak and corduroys. Digby was quite still. The man got up and greeted the dog. Digby scarcely reacted. There was some discussion amongst the humans while Digby sat, quivering with nervousness. Another woman came into the room and, after a further short period of talking, Digby's leash was removed. The man fished inside a carrier bag and took out a leather collar and lead. With some difficulty the collar was fitted around Digby's neck. The dog was so jumpy that the man took an age to get him ready. Then they were outside in the yard, walking towards the door that opened into the street.

Traffic thundered past in either direction. Digby's old fear returned and he reacted violently. The man's arm was nearly wrenched out of its socket as the dog tried to escape.

'Hey, wait on! Wait a moment,' the man called as he was dragged into an involuntary run. He pulled back on the lead. 'You don't need to do that. There's no danger. I'm going to look after you now. Don't worry, we'll soon be out of this.'

Digby licked his lips nervously. The man had a kind voice and Digby felt a little comforted. They proceeded into a quieter side street and the man marched along briskly. Digby was used to a lead and kept pace obediently. He was beginning to wonder if he was being taken to a new home. If so, it was unlikely to be the home he longed for.

The side street came out on to a major road where the traffic was at its worst. Digby hung back.

'No use doing that,' the man told him, dragging him slightly. 'We have to cross here.' He had to force Digby to the kerbside, and they waited by some traffic lights. Digby trembled. When the lights changed to red the other pedestrians walked swiftly across, but Digby had to be urged to move. The man succeeded in pulling him to the island in the middle of the road but Digby was now in a fever to escape and put on a spurt. It was too late for the man to stop him. With his arm at full stretch he was hauled into the path of traffic turning from the left. A car which had swung round the corner too fast braked with a screech, but the man was struck hard and knocked to the ground, his grip on Digby's lead automatically loosening. The dog galloped away, avoiding the converging vehicles by a hair's breadth, trailing the lead behind him.

All traffic came to a standstill as people rushed to the scene. The man in the road didn't move. One young boy, spotting the fleeing Digby, tried to stop the terrified dog by stamping on the trailing lead, but the collie only increased his breakneck speed and yanked the lead from beneath the lad's foot. Frantic now, Digby ran even faster, skidding into a side road at the first opportunity as his instinct guided him away from the din.

A young man walking on the other side of this road saw the dog race past. Realizing something was wrong, and afraid the collie might come to harm, he began to run after the dog. Digby was tiring, and after a few minutes the young man was able to grab him. Then something wonderful happened. The young man spoke, and Digby recognized the warm tones of friendship and sympathy instantly. This was the outsider who had talked to him so kindly in the Dogs' Home. Digby quivered with relief. He knew Frank and Frank knew him. They both felt they had found each other.

Frank had no idea how the dog came to be where he was, but it was clear that something had frightened him badly. He obviously couldn't be left to run free, and Frank felt it was up to him to take charge.

'Whatever it was that brought us together,' he told Digby, 'I think we were somehow meant for each other.'

Digby responded at once to his voice, wagging his tail and putting out his tongue to lick Frank's hand.

'We'll go home then,' said Frank. 'I know your name. I've had it in my mind ever since I saw it on the door of your pen. So, Digby, come with me now.' He took up the lead and gave it a wipe. 'That's it. Now we're ready. It's this way we want.'

They walked down a succession of residential streets, each one similar to the one before. Digby padded along, not even pausing to sniff. At length they came to a road called Keserly Street and arrived at a large Victorian house on the corner. It was almost the last of its kind in the neighbourhood where the huge old dwellings from another era had been steadily replaced by flats and smaller modern houses. This building had certainly seen better days. Many of the windows were cracked or broken. Some were boarded up. What paint was left around them was flaking. The front door had once been varnished but was now bleached and stained by weather. The brickwork was crumbling in several places, as was the path leading to the front door. What had once been a garden was now rampant with huge weeds and overgrown shrubs. Digby could smell a variety of human and canine scents. Already he could pick out Frank's among them. The strange odours, however, alarmed him. Frank pushed at the front door and it creaked open. There was no lock.

'In we go. Your new home,' he whispered to Digby.

A radio blared away somewhere upstairs. Frank released Digby from the lead and took him into a room that led off the hall. There was no carpet on the floor, only newspaper, and no curtains at the window. A broken table, a chair with a torn rush seat, and a number of orange-boxes and plastic milk crates stood about the room, these last holding Frank's few belongings. Against one wall lay a bare mattress, two skimpy blankets rolled up next to it. Frank sank on to the mattress and took a swig from a half-empty milk bottle that had been left on the table. Digby sat down, licking his lips. Frank looked at him for a moment. Then he jumped up, fetched a plastic bowl from one of the crates and poured some milk into it.

'Share and share alike, Digby,' he said kindly.

Digby wagged his tail and bent to drink. He lapped sloppily at the milk, which was not very fresh. The blaring radio suddenly stopped. There were footsteps on the stairs. An older man, bearded and long-haired and very unkempt, came into the room. A pungent smell hung about his grubby clothes, and Digby backed away.

'It's all right,' Frank said. 'Norman won't hurt you. I'll see to that.'

The man called Norman was looking, without much interest, at Digby.

'Where did you find him?' he asked gruffly.

Frank explained what had happened.

'You'll get some attention with that one,' Norman conceded. 'He'll draw the punters in all right.'

Frank frowned slightly. Digby was still looking nervous. 'I didn't just rescue him for money,' the young man declared. 'This is the dog I told you I liked at the Home. And he likes me, I can tell. We'll be great mates together, Digby and me.'

'You can never tell,' said Norman. 'Are you going out?'

'Later,' replied Frank. 'Where's Chip?'

'Upstairs.'

'Perhaps he'd better be introduced to Digby now. What do you think? It could be awkward when it gets dark.'

'Right you are.' Norman clumped up the bare wooden stairs and returned almost at once, holding a black and brown mongrel that looked something like a Manchester terrier by the scruff of its neck. Chip jumped forward eagerly, but Norman pulled him back. Digby stood his ground, his ears cocked. The dogs' tails showed their willingness to be friendly.

'No problem,' Norman grunted, walking Chip forward a little so that the dogs' noses could explore each other. 'They'll be fine.'

Digby was taller than Chip but Chip was bolder. As they assessed one another Digby thought of Streak for the first time since he had left the Dogs' Home. How dignified and superior he was compared to this cocky young mongrel.

'You're a classy one and no mistake,' Chip was muttering as he circled the collie. 'Don't know how you're going to make out. Street life's not what you're used to, I bet.'

'I don't know what you mean,' said Digby.

There was no time for explanations then because Norman was pulling Chip back again. Digby was left to puzzle over the other dog's remarks. Then he felt Frank's hand on his head, stroking along his neck to his shoulders, affectionately but firmly. Digby relaxed. As long as Frank was around he was sure he'd be all right.

Later that day Frank snapped Digby's lead on and took him out of the house. It was late afternoon and growing cool. Digby had had nothing to eat since leaving the Dogs' Home. His stomach rumbled. He had been used to a meal in the early afternoon in his pen. However, there didn't seem to be any prospect of food at present. Frank was walking along in a purposeful way. They came to a busier street where throngs of people were scurrying to and from a wide entrance between buildings. It was the beginning of the evening rush hour, and Frank was returning to one of his regular pitches outside an Underground station.

He made Digby sit down against a wall. Then he looped the end of the lead a couple of twists round one leg of his jeans and tied a loose knot before pulling a mouth-organ from his pocket and beginning to play. Digby didn't like the sound and laid his ears back. He wanted to run, but now he was on a short lead. Frank braced himself against Digby's tugging and continued to play. People hurried past without giving them a glance. Frank finished one tune and wrenched a crumpled cap from an inside pocket of his leather jacket. He dropped it to the pavement by his feet and fished around for his few remaining coins, which he dropped into the upturned cap. Then he started to play again.

Digby was hungry and miserable. He hated the sound of the music and, without Frank's comforting voice, began to feel neglected. He raised his head and howled. Now some of the passers-by glanced in their direction, amused by this odd duet. Coins started to tinkle into the cap to join the ones that Frank had put there. Digby howled louder. Frank seemed to have forgotten him. Frank blew and sucked harder to drown him out, but Digby reacted with ever more desperate cries of anguish. Many Underground travellers were laughing at the din. Frank watched the money lining his cap. It was mounting up nicely. He wanted to stop playing – Digby's howls were almost too upsetting – but he dared not while money was collecting like this.

'Oh, stop your moaning,' he pleaded after finishing

another tune. Digby's eyes begged for attention. Frank
squatted down and gave the dog a sympathetic hug.
'This is for your benefit too, you know,' he murmured.
'We're going to have a real good supper tonight.'

As the number of travellers dwindled Frank tucked
his mouth-organ away and counted up his takings. He
let out a low whistle. 'Well, you've earned your keep
already,' he declared. 'And you deserve a reward. I *knew*
we were right for each other.' He pocketed the change
hurriedly. 'Now we'll go and spend it!' he laughed.
'Otherwise it'll wear holes in my pockets.'

Spending the money was easy. Frank marched to a
nearby McDonald's and bought giant-size portions of
burgers and chips. The smell of the food had Digby,
waiting outside, drooling uncontrollably. Frank found
a bench by a little green, a short walk from the station.
There they shared the meal, Frank passing every other
piece of meat to Digby, who swallowed it gratefully.
When they had finished Frank said, 'Now we need to
buy some supplies.' He re-counted his money and set
off once again, this time to a small local supermarket.
There was enough money to buy bread, butter, milk,
cheese, apples, dog food, some canned drinks, and a
few tins of food that didn't need heating.

Back in the squat Frank arranged his provisions in
his boxes and put the bread, butter and milk on the
table.

'Are you thirsty?' he asked Digby. The dog thumped
his tail on the floor agreeably. He was quite happy
in these unusual surroundings. He had been fed and
exercised and was ready to fall in with anything Frank
might want to do. Frank poured some milk into a bowl.

'This is yours now,' he told the collie. 'It's Digby's
bowl. No one else must use it.' As Digby drank Frank
bent and stroked his soft coat. 'We're a team, aren't

we, you and I?' he crooned. 'We're best mates. We
don't need anyone else.'

Digby turned and licked Frank's hand, his warm
brown eyes seeking his young master's.

'Well!' said Frank softly. 'I believe you understand
every word I say to you.' He threw himself on to his
mattress and stretched out contentedly. 'There's room
for two here,' he offered, patting the side of the mattress invitingly. 'We'll keep each other warm.'

Digby needed no second bidding. He hastened to
the bed and the two snuggled down together. The
room wasn't entirely dark before they fell asleep.

4

During the night Frank and Digby were woken by a commotion in the hall. Norman, who had been out when they had returned earlier, came back. In the unlit house, he tripped over Chip who had been with him, and crashed to the floor. Chip yelped as Norman's heavy body fell almost on top of him.

'Damn the animal!' Norman swore. 'Will you get out of my way, you stupid dog?' There was a thump and another yelp. 'Serves you right! I'll give you another one if you don't clear off!' There followed a scrabbling noise. Chip was evidently trying to escape up the stairs. Suddenly Norman began singing in a loud but not unmelodic voice.

'Oh no,' Frank groaned, his hand smoothing Digby's taut body reassuringly. 'Someone's been buying him drinks. Now we'll get no peace.'

The singing was extraordinary. Norman veered from folk-song to pop to a ballad and back again. Frank held his head. Norman started on a hymn.

'This is too much, isn't it, Digby?' Frank jumped up and switched on a torch. 'Shut up!' he called, but Norman was well into his stride now and ignored him. Frank went out to the hall. 'Come on, now. Let's get you to your bed. You need to sleep. And so do we!' he added emphatically.

Norman was slumped against the wall. Frank put an arm round him and helped him to his feet. Chip was lying quietly at the top of the stairs.

'I don't want to sleep. I want to sing,' Norman protested.

'You'll wake everyone up.'

'Everyone? There is nobody. Only you and me. I can make as much noise as I like in a condemned house! Who's to stop me?'

'Now don't get belligerent,' Frank said. 'You're supposed to sing for your supper; not when you get home.'

'Home? Home, you say? This is no home to me. My home's a long way from here. My home's—'

'Shut *up*!' Frank snapped, losing his patience. He began to walk Norman to the stairs. 'Now, come on. Up this one. Now the next . . .'

Digby had followed Frank out and had grabbed Norman's trouser-bottom in his teeth. He tugged at it, growling mildly.

'Digby, you're not helping,' Frank told him. Cowed by the stern tone, Digby let go. Gradually, the two men advanced up the stairs. Digby stood at the bottom. Chip came to join him and began to yap rapidly.

'Noisy old cove, isn't he? He's often like this. He used to live on the streets. Like me. That's how I got to know him. He used to give me bits of bread. In the end I stayed with him. Your bloke – the young one – found us this place. Cosy, isn't it?'

Digby was unable to answer. He tried to compare the house and its relative comfort with the Dogs' Home. 'How long have you been in this place?' he asked.

'Doesn't seem long,' Chip said. 'What about you? You're no street dog.'

Digby began to explain about the Dogs' Home. He didn't get far.

'Oh! I know all about that,' Chip interrupted him. 'I've been in there. And out again. And back in. It's a game with some of us, isn't it? I didn't like it. Hemmed in there with blank walls and nowhere to run but round in a circle. I'll take this life any day. At least you can stretch your legs and use the senses you were born with.'

Digby didn't argue. 'But what about a *real* home? Wouldn't you like that better?'

'It's cosy enough here, isn't it?'

'No – I mean one where you get proper care and attention from your owner.'

'Owner? What do you mean? Nobody owns me.'

Digby was confused. 'Then why do you stay with the old man? If he's not—'

'Suits me. Suits him,' Chip answered. 'For now.'

'I had another home once,' Digby said. 'Quite unlike this one. It was—'

'Why didn't you stay there then?' Chip barked irritably. He thought Digby was trying to sound superior.

'I was . . . abandoned,' Digby muttered. There! He had said it. He had finally been able to admit the awful truth.

'Not so special, then, are you?' Chip sneered.

'I never claimed to be. I was only trying to explain.'

'All right. No harm done. Anyway, we're in the same groove now. Your bloke and my bloke and us two. Like a little family, aren't we?'

Digby didn't think so at all, but he kept quiet. Frank was coming downstairs again. Digby wagged his tail vigorously. Frank was all the family he wanted.

'All quiet now,' Frank said. 'Fast asleep. Come on, Digby. Let's get some rest. Goodnight, Chip.'

In the morning Frank was up bright and early. He took Digby for a quick run, then left him alone to go to the nearest public lavatory to wash and shave. Digby lay on the grubby mattress and pined. He had no way of knowing where Frank had gone or when he would come back. Chip came to join him but was no comfort.

'What's got into you?' the mongrel demanded. 'You look like a mouse in a cattery.'

Digby didn't answer. He was too miserable and nervous. He wished Chip would go away.

'You'll swallow your tongue in a minute if you keep gulping like that,' Chip mocked him.

Digby merely turned a wounded glance on the mongrel.

'Oh, look at those eyes,' Chip gibed. 'Enough to melt a heart of stone.'

In the end Digby's refusal to respond drove Chip away. The mongrel was bored and looked for stimulation elsewhere. He pattered upstairs to see if Norman was awake.

Digby had never felt so alone. In the Dogs' Home there had been almost constant noise. He had always been aware that his plight was shared by all the other dogs and that knowledge had provided a grain of comfort. And of course there had been Streak. How he wished Streak was with him now!

Digby was terrified that he had been abandoned again. The thought of it made him tremble. To be abandoned here would be a far worse fate than before. Where would he go? What would become of him? He might end up a street dog. He tried to think about Tam and Millie and that comfortable little world in which he had grown up, but the image of Frank was so much more vivid that it kept blotting the other world out. Had he lost Frank so soon after finding him? Digby began to howl. Not the way he had howled across Frank's music, but a heart-rending, eerie wail that sounded ghostly in the empty shell of the house.

Norman awoke with a start. 'What's that? What's that dreadful din?' he muttered, hardly conscious of where he was.

Digby's howls continued to pierce the musty silence

of the old man's wreck of a room. Norman staggered
out of the pile of greasy blankets that made his bed.
'Stop it! Stop that horrible row!' he roared, shaking
his head as though to blot out the noise. He had had
a nightmare and this unearthly sound seemed like a
continuation of it. Chip slunk into a corner. He could
recognize when Norman was in an ugly mood. Norman
steadied himself, blinking, and registered that the din
was coming from downstairs. Three wobbly strides took
him to the staircase. Cursing and muttering all kinds
of threats, the man started down.

'You'll stop that now or else I'll stop it for you,' he
bellowed as he lurched into Frank's room.

The collie wavered as Norman confronted him. But
Digby had frightened himself with his howls and now
he couldn't stop. Norman raised one arm and dealt
him a hefty blow.

'I warned you, didn't I, you stupid beast?' Norman
growled as Digby yelped in pain. Outside, Frank heard
the cry as he came up the broken path. He hurried
to the door.

'What are you doing?' he asked icily.

'Nothing at all.' Norman avoided his glance. 'I
thought I heard something . . .' He sounded uncon-
vincing.

'You heard something all right. And so did I.' Frank
saw Digby cowering on the mattress, looking from one
man to the other. As soon as the collie caught Frank's
gaze his tail began to bang up and down. Frank resisted
the urge to go to his dog at once. He glared at Norman,
who was fumbling with a broken button. 'If you've
been—'

'Honest to God, Frank,' Norman interrupted him
uneasily. 'He just got in the way, that's all. He—'

'You know what happened with Billy,' Frank said.
There was still a hard edge to his voice which prevented

Digby from running to him. 'Billy was a good dog. He ran away because of you. I don't want to lose this one. He's special.'

'He is. Of course he is. I know that. I wouldn't touch him. Look at his face. How could anyone?'

Frank pursed his lips. Norman stumbled away, calling over his shoulder, 'I'll be collecting my benefit later. Is there anything you need?'

'Only what you already owe me,' Frank grunted.

'You'll get it all,' Norman promised.

Now Frank turned to his dog. He crouched, opening his arms and calling softly. Digby rushed to him, his feelings exploding in a surge of delight. Wriggling and squealing with the sheer bliss of Frank's return, the collie knew now that Frank would never leave him. Frank would always come back.

Frank owned a stiff brush and he spent some time brushing Digby's coat. The collie, like all the dogs in the Home, had been well cared for and Frank wanted his dog to look clean and smart. When they went out Digby drew admiring glances and comments from passers-by. He was so full of confidence now that Frank looked after him that, little by little, things that had scared him before lost their ability to upset him. In particular, he became so used to traffic that the noise no longer frightened him. Frank always kept him on a lead for his own safety. The young man strode jauntily along with long, loose strides and Digby kept perfect pace with him, always at his side. They were almost never apart, so much so that Chip started to show resentment.

At night the two dogs sometimes met in the hall. Digby never showed any curiosity about what lay upstairs, but Chip was used to roaming all over the house. Downstairs, at the back, was a dilapidated

kitchen. Chip occasionally slept in there, keeping an
ear cocked for rats and mice. There was another room
too, opposite Frank's, but its door was kept closed
because the floor had collapsed. Chip had never been
in there but he often put his nose to the crack under
the door in a vain effort to discover what lay behind it.

'You ever been in there?' he asked Digby one night.

'No. Why should I?'

'No reason. I just asked,' Chip said irritably.

'The men never go in there, do they?'

'Nope. Aren't you even a bit inquisitive about it?'

'I can't say I am. My master and I have all we want
in the other place.'

'That's how you see him now, is it, "your master"?'

'Of course. Don't you?'

'I told you. Nobody owns me. And the young bloke
doesn't have much to do with me. He's a good friend,
though. I like him. My old bloke's all right if you keep
on the right side of him. Sometimes it's best to keep out
of the way. I understand him. But if he ever tried any
real funny business on me, I'd be off straight away.'

'Not so easy that, is it?' Digby said. 'Doesn't he keep
you on a lead?'

'Me? On a lead? You're joking!' Chip scoffed. 'Just
let him try!'

'It doesn't bother me. In fact I feel secure that way,'
Digby said.

'Oh, you two!' Chip exclaimed. 'Always together,
night and day. Don't you ever feel like wandering
around on your own?'

'I never liked being alone,' Digby replied. 'I always
had company. I was brought up with my brother. Didn't
I tell you about it?'

'Yeah. You told me.' Chip yawned. 'Doesn't always
pay to get too thick with a human. They can let you
down.'

'Yes. They can,' Digby admitted, thinking of how he had been lodged in the Home. 'It takes you an age to get over it. But I trust this one completely. He'll never fail me.'

'He's human, isn't he?' Chip mocked. 'I wouldn't be too sure, if I were you. He had another dog before.'

Digby was interested at once, even feeling a twinge of jealousy. 'What happened?' he asked eagerly.

'He weren't treated right. So he vamoosed.'

'Ran away?'

'Yeah. He was a poor-looking creature. Only small. A brown, rough-coated sort of mutt. Not enough flesh on him to feed a crow. He sort of fastened himself on my old bloke before I did. But he couldn't stand the winter weather. So the young bloke – your Mr Perfect – took pity on him and took him in here. Later, us two joined the happy family. The brown mutt, Billy, tried to worm his way back into the old gaffer's feelings. I didn't like that and we used to squabble and scrap. The old gaffer got so mad about it, he used to lash out. Mostly I was too quick and skipped out of the way. Billy wasn't so young or nimble. He caught a few prize wallops. And then he sort of forgot any training he might have had in the most basic thing. Couldn't control his waterworks. The old gaffer was madder than ever. He made Billy so miserable, the dog scarpered in the end.'

'Why didn't my master help?'

'He did try. But during the winter he weren't well. Spent most of the day lying on the floor. Seemed to be no fight in him.'

'And Billy? Where is he now?'

'Who knows? Never seen him again to this day,' Chip grunted. 'I doubt he survived.'

'Poor creature,' Digby said sadly.

'Yeah. He was. I believe that myself. But I wasn't

going to have my nose pushed out of joint. Now, you
and me – we don't cramp each other, do we? You keep
to your patch and me mine. We can get along.'

'Oh yes, we'll get along,' said Digby. 'Just so long as
we both remember where our loyalty lies.'

Chip eyed him for a moment or two. At the outset
he had taken Digby for a softie, but there was a new
confidence and firmness in his tone recently. Maybe
he wasn't such a pushover after all.

5

There were still a few houses in the street in good repair. Some were divided into flats, and in one of these lived a middle-aged woman on her own. She and Frank often saw each other and always exchanged a word or two. She had great sympathy for the young man and she was even more compassionate towards his dog. She imagined Digby had a very miserable time, although whenever she saw him he always looked well groomed and healthy. She thought he deserved a proper home, and one day she decided to say so.

Frank and Digby were returning in the evening from their pitch by the Underground station. By now, the dog that tried to howl a kind of duet with the man's harmonica was very well known and people gave regularly and generously to the collection. The duo had become a local attraction. The woman was on her way home from work, and their paths crossed.

'Good evening, Mr Farmer.'

'Evening, Miss Crisp. Are you well?'

'I am, thank you. Your dog looks tired. Has he been singing again?'

Frank chuckled. 'What passes for it. I think he really enjoys it now.'

'He's a lovely dog. Aren't you, Digby?' Miss Crisp bent to give the collie a pat. Digby submitted without enthusiasm. 'It's a pity to think,' she resumed, 'that you both have to go back to that cold, dark place.

'I'm working on that, Miss Crisp,' Frank assured her for the umpteenth time. Their conversations seemed generally to follow this pattern.

'I'm sure you are. But wouldn't you like the dog to have a more settled existence? *He* has no choice in the matter.'

Frank sighed. 'What did you have in mind?' He already knew the answer.

'I'd be thrilled to take him off your hands. I'm quite alone and I'd welcome the company.'

'I'm sure you would but, you see, we're a team. We—'

'I know, I understand,' the woman cut in. 'Digby's your meal ticket. Please. I don't mean to interfere. But just give it a thought. Things must be difficult enough for you without having an animal to feed and care for. You can be sure I'd pay well for him. He's worth a lot.'

'Oh dear. Look, I'm sorry,' Frank said. 'You're very kind. But I don't want the money. We make out well enough. I love Digby. He's all the world to me. And he's just as devoted, you know. How could I part with him?' He sounded upset.

Miss Crisp smiled wanly. 'I see,' she whispered. 'In that case, I wouldn't want to be the person to split you up. But remember, if ever you need anyone to act as a dog-sitter' – she gave a little laugh – 'you don't have to look any further than me. You know where I live.'

'That's most kind of you, Miss Crisp,' Frank replied warmly. 'I appreciate your offer, really I do.'

They went on their separate ways. The woman turned to look back once or twice. 'I believe that dog *will* come to me one day,' she murmured to herself.

There was a knot of people outside the squat, most of them neighbours. Frank soon discovered the reason. From inside the building Chip's anxious barking was clearly audible. Something was wrong.

'The dog's been going on like that for an hour or more,' said one man to Frank. 'It sounds distressed.'

'Why didn't you go in?' Frank asked. 'There's no lock on the door.'

'We didn't like to,' was the reply. 'We didn't know if the building was safe.'

Frank started to run up the path. 'That's just it,' he shouted. 'Some of it isn't!'

As soon as he had pushed the door open he realized what had happened. Chip stood in the hall, looking into the room that was usually kept closed. Norman lay, groaning faintly, at the bottom of a deep drop in what had once been the cellar of the house. He had crashed through the broken flooring in the unused room. Shattered floorboards stood up on end at crazy angles around a wide hole. Frank inched forward, as close as he dared.

'Norman!' he called. 'Norman! Can you hear me?'

The only reply was a long drawn out groan. Frank dashed outside again. 'Someone please call an ambulance! There's been an accident.'

Two men joined Frank in the overgrown garden. 'Is it the old fellow?' one asked. He knew Norman well by sight.

'Yes. He's fallen through the floor,' Frank answered. 'Probably had too much to drink again and lost his bearings. Went into the wrong room, the silly old fool! We *never* use that room.'

'Shouldn't use the house at all, if it's so dangerous,' the other neighbour commented. 'Is he badly hurt?'

'I don't know. It sounds like it.'

The ambulance arrived a quarter of an hour later. It was impossible to reach Norman from ground level indoors. There was an entrance to the cellar outside. The ambulance men had to break the door down. They found that the old man had broken a leg and smashed some ribs. He would have been in a much worse plight if he had landed on the concrete floor of the cellar.

Luckily some debris – empty cartons and old news-
papers – had cushioned his fall. Norman was whisked
off to hospital and Frank was left with the two dogs
and repeated warnings from all the onlookers about
remaining in such perilous surroundings.

'All right, dogs. All right,' said Frank when the three
of them were finally left alone. He flopped down on his
mattress and Chip came clambering over him, needing
consolation. Digby grumbled a little but Frank quietened him.

'You must be good boys, both of you,' he told the
dogs. 'I'll have to leave you for a while. I must find out
if poor Norman's OK and see if he needs anything.'
He gave them some food and ran upstairs to fetch
Norman's belongings. He left the radio and gathered
up a few odds and ends which he judged the old man
might want with him.

'He has less even than I do,' Frank mused, looking
round. He was moved by the starkness of Norman's
room. 'Not much to show at the end of your life . . .'

Left alone, Digby eyed Chip jealously. He didn't want
the mongrel to sleep on Frank's mattress and he
growled every time Chip tried to come near.

'Why hog it?' Chip complained.

'You've got your own bed,' Digby reminded him.
'This is mine.'

'I don't feel like being on my own just now.'

'Understandable. But stay where you are.'

They lay silent for a while. Then Chip said, 'The old
gaffer won't be back, I'm sure of it.'

Digby said, 'Why not? Where else can he go?'

'Nowhere. I think he's dying. What'll happen now?'

'My master will feed you,' Digby said confidently.

'Mr Perfect? Yes, I expect you're right. But he won't
want two dogs, will he?'

Digby seriously hoped not, though he didn't voice his thoughts.

'I'll be back on the street,' Chip said. 'Then it'll be the Home again. Just my luck.'

Digby's thoughts drifted to his pen in the Dogs' Home. He was reminded of Streak. Was he still there? He thought he probably was. 'If you see an elderly black greyhound, ask him his name,' he said. 'It might be Streak. He was good to me. Tell him—'

'Hold on, hold on, I'm not there yet,' Chip protested. 'Perhaps it won't be me going back in, perhaps it'll be you.' He glared at Digby resentfully.

Digby hadn't considered that possibility. He had believed he and Frank would be together for always. But there were two dogs now . . . He sat up. 'I hope you're not going to go fawning over my master, trying to ingratiate yourself,' he said. 'I don't intend to be supplanted.' There was a warning note in his voice. 'Remember Billy . . .'

Frank didn't know what to do about Chip. Norman was in a bad way and could be out of action for weeks. It was unlikely he would be discharged to roam the streets. Frank didn't have the heart to kick Chip out, but he had to leave him behind when he and Digby went out collecting. He struggled to feed them both and now Chip spent all his time in Frank's room. The solution to the problem was eventually taken out of Frank's hands.

One sunny morning he took Digby to a local park. He had exercised Chip earlier; he didn't like walking the two dogs together, one on a lead and one off. In the park Frank came across a group of young homeless people, some of whom he knew well. It was a warm day and they were sitting on the grass together, drinking canned beer and swapping stories. Frank joined them,

only too grateful for some jolly human company. Digby
lay at his feet, content to drowse in the sunshine. One
tale led to another and time passed quickly. Some of
the others brought out some food and shared it
around. The afternoon wore on, and by the time Frank
pulled himself away to return home the sun was beginning to sink.

As they turned the corner of their street both he and
Digby sensed that something had changed. The place
somehow felt different. Frank suddenly stood stock still.
'It's gone!' he gasped. 'The squat's gone!'

Digby caught his sense of shock and trembled. Miss
Crisp ran out from her flat and grabbed Frank's free
hand. 'You poor love,' she said. 'The council have sent
in the demolition men. The house was a danger, Frank,
it's been condemned for years. It had to go.'

Frank groped for an answer. 'Yes . . . I know. It was
bound to happen . . . I just didn't expect it now . . . My
things!'

A man mowing his lawn called out, 'Good riddance,
I say. It was a stain on the neighbourhood. Decent area
like this. We don't want your kind round here!' Frank
didn't hear him. He wanted to rescue what he could.
But there was nothing left. Only piles of bricks and
timbers and tiles. His possessions, scanty as they were,
were buried under tons of dust and rubble. Amazingly,
Norman's radio had escaped damage. It stood forlornly
on a broken brick near the path. Perhaps one of the
workmen had saved it.

Miss Crisp, panting a little, had followed Frank to
the ruin. 'The other dog ran off,' she said. 'There was
no catching him.'

Frank blinked dazedly, trying to grasp her words.
'Oh,' he said finally. 'Chip's gone, then. We're on our
own, Digby. And we've nothing left.'

6

'Wherever will you go?' Miss Crisp asked. 'Is there a hostel somewhere?'

'Not one where I could guarantee to get a bed,' Frank answered. 'And they wouldn't allow Digby in. I'll find a sheltered doorway somewhere. That's all I can hope for now, and it won't be the first time.'

Miss Crisp wrung her hands. 'Must it be like that? Don't you have family?'

Frank grimaced. 'I'd rather not talk about them,' he said. He seemed to shut the thought away. 'You know, I had some hopes of getting a job,' he continued. 'They wanted a barman at a pub in Berlin Road. Not too fussy there – I could have given my address as 38 Keserly Street. But 38 Keserly Street has been razed to the ground.' He turned and looked regretfully again at the pile of rubble that had once been home to him.

'Would these pub people know that?' Miss Crisp hinted.

'No, they wouldn't necessarily. But there's a difference,' Frank explained. 'I could keep myself halfway decent in there' – he jerked his thumb at the ruin – 'with a roof over my head. I can't do that sleeping rough. So they won't want to know.'

'I'm so sorry, I really am,' Miss Crisp went on. 'I can help you with food . . . and even shelter for a bit if you wish. I don't like to think of you reduced to begging.'

'Miss Crisp, you're a wonderful person,' Frank said. 'But I wouldn't dream of being a burden. And as for begging – what else have I been doing for months?'

'It's not begging if you're playing music, is it?'

'Some would say so.'

'Is there nothing I can do for you?'

Frank glanced at Digby. 'There is one thing,' he answered. 'I need to look for a bolt-hole for tonight. I don't want to drag the poor dog around with me. Could you take Digby for a few hours?'

Miss Crisp's face lit up. 'What do *you* think? It would be a pleasure.'

'I'm so grateful to you.' Frank ran a hand through his hair. He seemed a little desperate. He passed Digby's lead to the woman. 'Don't worry if I don't come for a while,' he told her. 'I'll be back at the latest tomorrow morning.' He squatted down and gave Digby a cuddle, talking to him about where he was going and when he would be back. Digby shivered. He knew Frank was parting from him. He licked Frank's hands and face in helpless sympathy. Miss Crisp had to haul the dog away.

Frank watched their retreating figures. Then he stepped back into the ruined garden. The edge of his old mattress protruded from a pile of debris. That would have to be sacrificed, but he badly needed to retrieve a blanket or two.

'I'm at rock bottom now,' he sighed to himself. He pulled a couple of torn stained blankets from among the rubbish. 'These'll hardly keep me warm tonight.' He collected Norman's radio and turned his back on the sorry scene. 'Lucky Norman,' he murmured. 'Warm and cosy in his hospital bed.'

There was nothing to do now but walk the streets until dusk. He had some money left and there was enough for a proper meal. While he ate it he thought about Digby. He knew the collie wouldn't be happy in Miss Crisp's flat. Perhaps he was already pining for him.

Digby was indeed feeling wretched. Despite the

woman's kindness, all he wanted to do was to get away. He ignored the food she fetched for him and lurked by the door, listening for the reassuring sound of Frank's footsteps and trying to detect the first familiar scent. He was disappointed. Although he was sure Frank wouldn't desert him, he didn't like Miss Crisp and growled every time she came too close.

'You don't meant that,' Miss Crisp cooed. 'You're just anxious for young Frank. You've nothing to fear from me. And he'll be back just as soon as he's ready for you.'

Digby didn't even turn to look at her. His mind was set on one thing: getting through that door. Miss Crisp couldn't budge him from the spot, so she at last decided to slip him on the lead and walk him in the open air. It seemed to her that if she could prove to Digby that Frank wasn't hanging around somewhere just outside, he would settle down.

Digby leapt through the open door like a thing possessed. Miss Crisp hadn't the strength to hold him. The lead caught on the door handle and snapped, and Digby bolted. The woman called in vain as the collie galloped first to the ruin of the squat and from there to the next most likely place where he thought Frank might be: the Underground station.

Frank wasn't there and Digby began to feel alarmed. He galloped down street after street, avenue after avenue, each road being one they had walked together at various times. But Frank had headed for the centre of the city, which Digby had never visited, and the collie saw no trace of him. He finished up searching the park where he and Frank had encountered the homeless group only hours earlier. The youngsters had dispersed but Digby came face to face with another acquaintance: Chip.

The mongrel was lying against a park bench which

was still slightly warm from the sun's rays, now completely disappeared. He looked very jaded and showed no pleasure, nor even surprise, as Digby cantered towards him.

'Have you seen him?' Digby began at once, panting heavily.

'Him? Who's "him"?'

'My master, of course. We were here earlier. Have you seen him, Chip?'

'Not today, I haven't,' the mongrel replied. 'And don't think I'm going to join in a search for him either. I'm going to stay here, nice and quiet, until someone carts me off to the Home.'

'You don't mean that!' Digby exclaimed. 'That's not what you want, I know. And supposing you're just left here? Supposing you're not picked up?'

'The park keepers know me from way back,' Chip explained wearily. 'If one of them's still around, he'll know what to do with me.'

'Don't give up,' Digby pleaded, beginning to feel afraid that the same fate might be awaiting him. 'We can find my master again. He'll always look after us.'

'How did you lose him?' Chip asked without much interest.

'He gave me to another human,' Digby answered. 'She took me indoors but I managed to get free.'

'More fool you,' Chip grunted. 'You should have stayed put. *I* would have. Mr Perfect won't know where you are now. If he wants to come back to you, how will he find you?'

Digby slumped belly-down on the grass. For the first time he understood that he had done the worst possible thing. He whispered, 'Then *we* must find *him*.'

'What do you mean, "we"?' Chip snapped. 'I told you. I'm staying right here.'

'Oh, Chip, won't you help me?' Digby begged. 'You

know how to get around. I can see I've been stupid; I need your street wisdom. You're an old hand at this sort of thing, aren't you? And you could benefit too.'

Chip glared back. 'I'm too tired, too old and too bored by the prospect,' he growled.

'My master's our only hope,' Digby whined. 'You can't give up like this! And you're not old. You always had plenty of bounce before.'

Chip yawned, but then he got slowly to his feet. He stretched his front legs and then his back. 'OK. You've convinced me,' he muttered. 'I'm a soft-hearted mutt, as you know. I won't leave you completely in the lurch.'

'You're a pal!' Digby yapped happily. 'I know we had some differences before. But now we can work together. We have the same purpose.'

'Yeah. Well, the first thing is to scarper from this park, because if we stay here we'll *both* find ourselves back in the compound.' Chip set off at an easy lope, keeping as much as possible away from the open expanse of grass. He led Digby through a shrubbery and under some tall trees, then alongside a wall until they could leave the park by a side exit.

'That was well done,' Chip congratulated himself. 'I haven't lost all my wits. Where to now?'

'Where? Oh, dear, I've no idea. What do you suggest? Where do humans go who have no home?'

'Same place as homeless dogs and cats. Come on – I know where a lot of them go, anyway.'

In a dark doorway in one of the main city streets Frank had wrapped himself in his two torn blankets. He had chosen a place in a row of shops, now closed up and deserted until the morning. Norman's radio was next to him. The batteries were failing but Frank could still hear the faint strains of a ballad he knew well. He had the volume control at its full extent. In an hour or

two there would be no sound at all. He took out his
harmonica and, blowing softly, followed the tune along.
The night was cloudy and not too cold. A few spots of
rain fell on the pavement in front of him. Frank wrig-
gled further into the doorway and pressed his back
against the closed door of a video hire shop. Few
people passed by and none of them gave him a second
glance. Frank knew that if he had had Digby with him
they would have been much more likely to show
interest. He sucked and blew, blew and sucked, in time
with the warbling voice. The song finished and a disc
jockey began to gabble. Frank played another tune and
wondered what the time was. It was going to be a long
night.

Chip led Digby along a main thoroughfare. They had
come a long way and it was late. Traffic along the road
was light. In every doorway one or two people had
bedded down for the night. Some had a blanket or rug
draped round them. Others had the luxury of a
sleeping-bag to snuggle into. Most were still awake.
Many of these people were accompanied by dogs, all
of which appeared to be related. They were all black
and brown dogs similar to Chip. Chip recognized a
few of them and greeted them curtly. Digby kept his
distance, unsure of the animals' temperaments. It was
soon clear that Frank wasn't occupying any of these
doorways. They came to a standstill.

'Now what?' Digby asked morosely. 'I don't think
we'll ever find him.'

'Hm! You give up too easily,' Chip told him. 'There
are loads of places we can search.'

Digby sat on his haunches. 'I'm tired,' he said.

'Yeah. We'll have a little rest,' Chip agreed. He lay
down on the pavement just where he was. After a
moment's hesitation Digby joined him.

'I'm back where I started,' Chip commented. 'I was born on the streets and I suppose I'll die on 'em.'

'But you must have had a home once,' Digby remarked wearily. 'You were in the compound more than once. You told me. So some kind human must have come and chosen you the first time? Someone like—'

'Your Mr Perfect?' Chip finished for him. 'Yeah. Someone came for me all right. An old biddy who wanted a bit of company. I was with her for a little. Then she died. So – back in I went.'

'And last time?'

'Last time was worse. I was put with a family. The children didn't understand me. They thought I was a toy or something. Teasing, humiliating, it went on and on. Even the adult humans could see it was no good. They packed me off to the dear old compound again. But I could see where I was heading and I thought, "Not this time, you don't!" And I escaped and that was it. Until I got in with the old bloke you know about. Life on the streets ain't so bad. At least you're not confined.'

'I don't want to live like that,' Digby said vehemently. 'I must find my master! I'm used to being cared for.'

'I know.' Chip was almost sympathetic. 'We'll keep looking and if two dogs aren't too much for him I might join you for a while. But it couldn't be for long. Too much to expect us to get along like that for good, eh?'

'I suppose you're right,' Digby said. 'You're very honest.'

'Honest, realistic, call it what you like. And— Whoops! Look out!' Chip barked a sudden note of warning, springing to his feet as he did so.

Digby looked round. A big man who had been slumped in one of the doorways had stirred, probably woken by the dogs' noise. He towered over the collie and, just before Digby sensed the danger he was in, lunged for the dog's collar and yanked Digby brutally towards him. Chip darted away with Digby's horrified yelps echoing in his ears.

'Shut yer row,' the big man growled. 'I don't know where you came from but you're just what I need. I could do very well out of you.'

7

After an uncomfortable and lonely night, Frank rolled up his blankets, picked up Norman's radio and set off for the usual place for a clean-up. He had lost his toothbrush and razor but at least there was soap on tap in the washroom. He felt a little better after sluicing his face and hands with warm water, but he was cold and stiff from his night on the pavement and he had hardly slept at all. Depressed, he made his way to Keserly Street.

Miss Crisp opened her flat door to him white-faced.

'Whatever's the matter?' Frank asked at once.

'I've lost him. He was so desperate to get away he just . . . wrenched himself free, and off he went.'

Frank's one consolation, his anticipation of being reunited with his dog, vanished in a flash. 'Oh no! How could you let that happen?' he said accusingly. Then, seeing Miss Crisp's distress, Frank recovered his usual good manners. 'I'm sorry. I shouldn't have put the responsibility on you. I didn't mean to . . .' He broke off with a woeful shake of his head.

'I've told the police,' Miss Crisp said. 'I said Digby was mine. I didn't know what else to do.' She noticed his pinched features. 'Oh, Frank, come in. Have some hot porridge and tea. You look frozen. And you can ditch those ragged things!' She pointed to the frayed blankets. 'I've plenty better here and you're welcome to any of them. And a cushion or two. I've an old holdall we can put things in for you.'

Frank allowed himself to be fussed over. It felt wonderful. He sank into a chair in the kitchen. The room

was so warm he started nodding at once, while Miss
Crisp bustled about. She brought him porridge and
toast and eggs and a pot of tea.

'There's more where that came from if you're still
hungry afterwards,' she told him. She was enjoying
herself too. It was a new experience for her to be
waiting on a young man.

'You're so good,' Frank kept saying between mouth-
fuls. 'I hope I don't mess your kitchen up with my dirty
things.'

'And that's another thing. You need some more
clothes,' she told him. 'Don't you qualify for an allow-
ance of some kind?'

'I don't take anything,' Frank replied proudly. He
groped in a pocket and brought out his mouth-organ.
'Here's how I earn my crust.'

'I know all about that,' Miss Crisp said. 'But you need
smartening up. Get yourself a proper job and digs. You
should accept what's due to you.'

Frank smiled. 'I'll do it in my own way,' he told her
gently. 'But let's talk about Digby. Have you any idea
which way he was heading? I must get him back.'

Miss Crisp told him all she knew. Frank noticed
Digby's broken lead dangling from a hook on the door.
He finished his breakfast and stood up. Miss Crisp
brought him the holdall as promised. 'How will I know
how to reach you if I hear from the police?' she asked.

'I'll keep in touch,' Frank said. 'Can you scribble
your phone number down for me?'

They parted, Frank expressing his gratitude. It wasn't
until quite a while later that he actually opened the
bag to see what was in it. The first thing that caught
his eye was a ten-pound note folded in half right on
top of the other items. 'Bless you,' he murmured.
There were two blankets, a small cushion, a towel, a
packet of soap tablets, a carton of toothpaste and

a large bar of chocolate. 'I'll pay you back one day, you dear woman,' he murmured aloud. 'You'll see.'

He had no clear idea of where Digby would have gone, since he was well aware that most of the surrounding area was unknown territory to the collie.

'I'll go down the roads he *does* know to begin with,' he told himself. 'There are quite a few people who've seen Digby with me by the station, so there's a good chance someone will have recognized him.'

Unfortunately, the man who had grabbed Digby was no well-wisher. He viewed the dog's crossing his path as a piece of luck and he meant to hang on to him. He knew where to go to get a good price for a healthy young collie like Digby. There was a market for dogs like him and unscrupulous black market operators could undercut professional breeders' prices without fear of an investigation.

'What are you going to do with him, Ken?' one of the big man's doorway neighbours called.

'I dunno yet,' came the grudging answer as the man peered down at the trembling collie. 'It needs some thinking about. I hope he's a pedigree.'

'How would you know?'

'I wouldn't. I mean to pass him off as such.'

'Aren't you going to keep him, then?'

Ken laughed a gravelly laugh low in his throat. 'What, pay out money to keep him fed and watered? You must be joking. I intend him to make me money, not cost me.'

'You'll have to feed him in the meantime.'

'We'll see about that, Denis,' the big man growled. 'I'm not going to be out of pocket for *him.*' He squatted down, wheezing with the effort, and gave Digby a thorough examination, pinching the dog's sides and belly.

Digby yelped. 'No, he don't need feeding,' Ken said categorically. 'He's fat enough.'

Before the night was over Ken had moved Digby out of sight. In that part of the city there was always an empty shed or a derelict building where a dog could be tied up and none the wiser. Ken replaced the useless remnant of Digby's lead with a serviceable piece of string and left him without a qualm, not even thinking to provide a container of water. His mind was occupied with one thought: how to pass the collie on as quickly as possible and take his cut. He made the necessary contact and arranged for pick-up the next evening.

During the day the shed in which Digby had been dumped grew very hot. The roof was made of corrugated iron and the spring sun beat down on it hour after hour. Digby had a raging thirst and there was not even a muddy puddle from which to quench it. He panted endlessly, suffering not only the torment of heat and thirst but also that of despair. He could think of nothing but Frank. Would his master be able to find him? Would he rescue him from the horrible man who had captured him? All day he lay on dry, stony ground longing for the young man to stride in, release him and whisk him away. Digby recognized once again the fatal error he had made in running from the kind woman's house. Unfamiliar as that had been, how much worse was this dreadful place! At last, worn out by his miserable captivity, he fell asleep.

There was a ray of hope for Digby. Chip had witnessed his capture. Although he had fled instinctively, the mongrel had crept back to the spot later the same night. Ken and Digby were no longer around, but Chip could follow a scent as well as any dog and set himself on their trail. Every now and again the scent mingled with so many others that it took Chip a while to disentangle the one he wanted from the rest, so it was far into the day when his nose finally led him to Digby's hiding-place. Chip was well pleased with himself when he peeped inside and saw the collie stretched out on the ground before him. He couldn't have told himself why he had acted in the way he had. And the sight of Digby lying alone in the shed made Chip experience something very unusual for him: a feeling of pity.

'There you are then,' he said awkwardly.

Digby woke at once and gave a squeal of delight. 'Chip! How did you find me?'

'Lying flat out,' Chip joked.

Digby barked. 'There's no time for humour. Have you seen my master?'

'Mr Perfect? No. I just followed my nose. I – I'm sorry I ran away, Digby. I didn't mean to desert you. I couldn't help myself.'

'It's all right.' Digby swallowed hard. 'Chip, I'm almost dying of thirst. There's no water here. Please fetch my master and get me out of here. The man tied me up. I can barely move at all.'

'Find him?' Chip echoed. 'Easier said than done, y'see, Digby. I mean – we don't know where he is, do we?'

'I've been thinking,' Digby gasped. 'If you go back to where he left me, he's bound to return there some time. Perhaps he's there now.'

'Where *did* he leave you?'

'Not far from where we were all living together. Farther down that road towards the corner. I can't remember much more about it. Another human – a female one – lives there. She took me in.'

'Oh yeah? That tells me a lot,' Chip commented sarcastically. But he could see Digby really was suffering. 'All right. I'll do what I can. If I see him, I'll try to make him understand. He must be worried about you.'

The thought made Digby more miserable than ever,

and he howled piteously. Chip made haste to leave. 'All's not lost yet,' he said encouragingly. '*I'm* still free to come and go.'

'But be quick, Chip,' Digby begged. 'The man might come back. Run as fast as you can!'

'I'm off!'

It was comparatively easy for Chip to find his way back to Keserly Street. But at that time of day a dog running free in city streets was an uncommon sight and one which attracted attention. Chip was well aware of this and tried to keep away from the main thoroughfares. The last thing he wanted now was for some well-meaning human to pounce on him in the belief that he was someone's lost pet. There was, moreover, the danger from traffic, at its height just then, and Chip needed to be particularly careful. He hated crossing roads in the daylight hours, but it was unavoidable. Digby was depending on him.

He had learnt that human pedestrians stood together in little groups at the roadside, waiting for motor traffic to come to a halt, when they wished to cross. He stood amongst them, warily watching for their reactions, and then, when they began to move, he darted across and put as much distance between him and them as he could as soon as he was safe. At all other times he kept well away from them, using kerbs and gutters in quiet roads to run along and brushing close to walls where it was sensible to avoid detection. He knew he drew comments and exclamations as he made his way along, but whenever a human cry was directed at him he broke into a loping run and soon was lost from view.

The familiar buildings of Keserly Street came into sight. Chip ran past the demolished house where he and Digby had lived uneasily together. The mongrel understood the situation was quite different now. Without any definite intention on his part they had somehow become friends. Chip thought of Norman and wished he might see him again. But then he spied the unmistakable figure of Frank ahead, in conversation with a woman, and all else was forgotten.

'No, I've heard nothing, I'm afraid,' Miss Crisp was saying. Frank had returned to her flat in the flimsy hope that the police might have contacted her while he had been searching the likeliest spots in the local area for Digby. He had drawn a blank himself. 'I've written out a "missing" notice,' Miss Crisp went on, 'with my telephone number on it. I'm going to take photocopies of it at work and then I can stick them on lamp-posts and telephone poles in some of the roads round here. You can take a look at it.'

Frank read the piece of paper she handed to him.

LOST. Welsh Border Collie, about three years old.
Wearing blue leather collar. If found, please
contact police or telephone 0171–675 1179.
Reward.

'A reward?' He whistled. 'You'd do that – for my dog?'

'He's worth it, isn't he?'

'Yes, but why should—Chip!' Frank suddenly cried out. 'Hello, boy! Oh, this is great. Look, Miss Crisp. Here's the other dog from my squat!'

Chip was demonstrating a mixture of delight and impatience, waltzing around Frank with his tail thrashing, but at the same time muttering little cries of exasperation.

'If Chip's come back,' Frank said eagerly, 'then maybe Digby isn't far behind?' He scanned the road, shading his eyes from the setting sun.

'I think he's trying to tell you something,' Miss Crisp said sharply. 'Look how he's pawing you.'

Chip was clawing at Frank's jeans and now began to bark. He ran off a little way and then turned, still barking insistently. Frank understood. 'All right, Chip, I'm coming!' He grinned at Miss Crisp.' I think this is it! I think he's found Digby!' He dropped the holdall and dashed off.

At that moment Digby was in such distress that he would almost have welcomed the return of Ken if he had been carrying a bowl of water. Shadows had crept into the shed and the temperature, mercifully, began to fall. Digby drooped, his head between his paws. Every now and then he lifted an ear as he caught the sound of footsteps nearby. But nobody appeared and he was left to fret at Chip's long absence.

At last he heard some scuffling as someone surreptitiously entered the shed. Digby was immediately alert and on his feet as he recognized the wheezing breaths of Ken. He drew back as the big man approached.

'That's good,' the man panted, relieved to see the dog was still where he had left him. However, even Ken could see the collie was in great discomfort. The dog's sides heaved and he trembled violently. Ken looked round for something which would hold water. He wasn't concerned on his own account, but he knew that the handler who was coming to fetch the collie would be angry if he should find him in this state. But there was nothing, not even a tin lid.

'You'd better stop that shuddering,' Ken growled. 'What d'you think you look like?' Digby shuddered all the more at the man's tone of voice. Ken shook his head and muttered, 'Wish I'd left a pail of water or something.'

It was too late. A car drew up outside. A door

slammed and there were more footsteps. Ken stood in front of Digby, hoping to screen the dog's suffering as far as possible from the other man.

'Hello, Mr Green.'

'Hi.' A tall thin man wearing an anorak entered the shed, and stared at Ken until he shuffled out of the way. Digby recoiled. 'How long's he been in here?' the man demanded.

'Since last night, Mr Green.'

'On his own?'

'Yes. I – I think he may need something to drink. I forgot to—'

'May need!' exclaimed Green. 'He looks all in. You don't give a toss about it, do you?'

'Well, yes,' Ken began.

'No, you don't!' Green interjected. 'I know you of old. All right, what did we say? Twenty-five?'

'Er – it was going to be more. He's a pedigree; you can see that.'

'I can't see anything of the sort in here,' Green said. 'And how do *you* know he is? Are you an expert suddenly?' He shook his head and swore. 'You haven't kept him properly. I'm not paying a penny more than I said.'

'You said forty on the phone.'

'Yeah. If he was up to standard. He's not.' Green began counting out five-pound notes. Ken was desperate for money and had no option but to take what was offered. Grumbling beneath his breath, he took the notes. Green untied Digby who hung back, digging in his heels, so that he had to be hauled outside.

As Green opened the car door another dog barked from nearby. There was the sound of someone running towards them. The two men glanced up as Chip came galloping along the road with Frank in hot pursuit. Green bundled Digby into the back of the car and jumped into the driving seat. Ken looked worried and tried to climb in the other side.

'You're not required,' Green snapped and pushed him away, at the same time starting the engine.

Frank started to shout as he saw Chip dancing round the car. The mongrel was in a fever of excitement. Green ignored the dog and put the car into gear. Frank raced up and just managed to wrench Chip clear as the car moved away. He saw Digby lurch across the back seat and yelled 'Stop!' It was useless. The car disappeared down the road while Ken took advantage of Frank's anguish to make himself scarce.

The young man still held Miss Crisp's 'missing' note in his hand. His eyes filled with tears as he re-read it. 'Lost,' he whispered. 'Yes, well and truly lost now. Lost for good.'

8

In the car, Digby's frantic barks were distracting the driver. The collie was leaping about from one seat to another in a kind of frenzy, and Green knew the dog had to be secured before he caused an accident. He drove slowly, looking for a place to park.

Green was not a black marketeer. He merely acted as the source of supply, acquiring stolen dogs, lost dogs, dogs from unlicensed breeders, and passing them on to the usual dealer. What happened to them then he didn't know and he didn't want to know. He made sure he had the responsibility of the dogs for as short a time as possible. He wasn't cruel to them and he didn't mistreat them. They were the commodity from which he made his money.

Eventually he spotted a gap ahead and eased his car into it. The pavements were quiet; a jogger in a track-suit was the only figure visible in the distance. Green jumped out and went round to the back. He drew on a pair of gloves. He was quite used to dogs attempting to bite him. Cautiously he prised open one of the rear doors. Digby growled at him savagely. Green made a grab for the string that was still attached to the dog's collar. He pulled it up short and looped it round the inside door handle, fastening it tightly and forcing Digby to the floor of the car. There were only twenty centimetres or so of slack and the collie could barely turn round.

'That's sorted you,' Green commented with satisfaction. He slammed the car door, then hesitated. A pub sign was illuminated a little way away. Green glanced back at Digby, remembering the dog had had nothing to drink for nearly twenty-four hours. He locked the car and hurried off to the pub.

'Do me a favour, will you?' he asked the barman. 'My dog's in a bit of a state. We've been in the car a long time and he needs a drink. Can you give me a bowl of water for him? And I'll have a beer myself.'

The barman was quite happy to oblige. While he went to fetch the water Green swiftly gulped down a glass of light ale. Then he carried the bowl back to the car, opened the door on the road side and placed the bowl on the floor.

Digby was in a fever to get at it. He twisted round from his position by the opposite door handle and strained with all his might to reach the water. However, Green had left the free part of the string so short that he couldn't quite make it. It was torture to see and scent the water but not be able to reach it, and Digby was driven nearly mad. With one supreme effort he yanked at the string, which tightened so suddenly round his neck that he was all but strangled. He slumped down, momentarily immobilized, but just as Green was about to lean further into the car to move the water nearer a lorry approached. The man had no choice but to slam the car door and flatten himself against it to enable the vehicle to pass. Meanwhile, Digby recovered slightly and once more in sheer desperation lurched for the water. The string, already dangerously tight, tightened some more and this time Digby collapsed completely. By the time Green was able to get to him the collie was merely a limp body on the floor of the car.

Green swore vehemently. Digby's eyes were bulging and his tongue protruded from his mouth. Green quickly loosened the string and untied it but it

appeared to be too late. The dog let out a long gasp
and lay still.

Green returned to the driver's seat. He drove off slowly,
looking for a place where the dog's body could be
dumped without suspicion. After a while he came to a
triangle of grass bordered by plane trees. There were
a couple of park benches by a path, and the area
was suitably shadowy. He stopped the car, and Digby was
soon in his arms. The dog hung slackly as Green carried
him towards one of the benches, but all at once he
stirred slightly and started to take some gasping
breaths. Green was surprised to find himself experien-
cing a sense of relief. But it made no difference now.

He was bending to deposit the collie under the
nearest bench when he noticed that the farther seat
had a puddle of water under it. 'I can do that much
for him anyway,' he told himself and straightened
again. He carried the dog to the far bench and laid
him underneath. 'That's it,' he said aloud, dusting his
hands. He was soon on his way again.

The cool night air revived Digby after a while. He
staggered to his feet, still breathing painfully. He saw
the puddle and sank his muzzle into it, lapping
greedily. The water made him cough and swallowing
was agony, but gradually the liquid soothed his throat.
Digby drank his fill and lay down again. He was very
tired, and felt very alone. He had no way of knowing
whether Green or the repulsive Ken was likely to
return. He didn't understand what had happened; why
he had been so tormented. He had no strength left
and was far too weary to make his escape, and soon he
fell asleep.

Digby awoke to find a grey cat sniffing at him. He got
to his feet. The cat stood his ground, sensing that the

dog was no threat. He watched the collie slake his thirst a second time from the puddle, and then the animals eyed each other.

'I'm as dry as dust,' Digby said. His voice rasped. He lifted a foreleg and scratched at his collar with a paw. 'I wish I could get this off. It does chafe so. My poor throat!'

'Have you been in a fight?' the cat asked.

'No. Much worse.'

'What happened?'

'Oh!' Digby gasped. 'Do you really want to know? It pains me to talk right now.'

'Suit yourself,' the cat replied. 'I'm not bothered.'

'I've got to get away,' Digby fretted. 'They might come back. But I don't know where to go.'

'Who might come back?'

'The men.'

'Have you run away?'

'No.' Then Digby remembered how the nightmare had begun. 'Well – yes, I did to begin with. I lost my master. And then – then the men came and snatched me. My master tried to rescue me, but . . .' Digby sank to the ground again. He was still very weak and his stomach was as hollow as a drum.

The cat stared at him. 'You're not making much sense,' he said flatly. 'You lost your master but he tried to rescue you? How's that possible? You dogs are all the same. You let humans run your lives for you. You can't turn round without them giving their permission first. I'm not surprised you end up bamboozled by them.'

Digby wasn't up to an argument. He saw the cat was about to leave him. 'Before you go,' he croaked, 'can you tell me if there's anywhere to hide round here? I must get away from this place.'

The cat considered. 'You'd better follow me then,' he advised.

Digby heaved himself upright. The cat eyed him critically. 'Are you sure you can manage it?'

'I'll try. I have to. Oh, if only there was something I could eat! I'm starving.'

'Don't look at me,' the cat said, ready to run.

'You're quite safe,' Digby told the animal. 'I'm not a hunter.'

The cat led off across the little park, crossed the empty road and snaked through a wrought-iron garden gate. Digby kept him within sight but was flummoxed by the gate. He was too big to pass through it as the cat had done, and far too weak to attempt a jump. He sat down on the pavement. The cat seemed to have disappeared.

'That's it, then,' Digby decided. 'I'll have to do the best I can for myself. There's no one to help me.' Suddenly the cat's head bobbed up between some plants in the garden. 'I can't get through here,' Digby explained rather irritably.

'Of course. I forgot your shortcomings for a moment,' the cat answered. 'It doesn't matter. There's another way.' She jumped on to the garden fence and stepped skilfully along its narrow top to another gate. This one was wooden. 'You can climb, I suppose?'

Digby was angry now. 'Are you taunting me? Can I climb?' he snapped. 'Have you ever seen a dog climb anything?'

'No. Another shortcoming, I believe,' the cat remarked, stretching his forelegs. 'You dogs haven't many accomplishments, have you? I can't think what humans see in you. Except they like to have a pet they can boss around.'

Digby growled with exasperation. 'What did you lead me to this dead end for?' he demanded.

'Give the gate a shove,' said the cat. 'Even Streak can do that.'

Digby froze. 'Streak?' he gasped.

'The dog here. The humans *had* to have a dog. Disrupting *my* life!'

Digby began to see why the cat objected to dogs so much. 'What sort of dog is it?'

'What sort? What sort is there?' the cat returned contemptuously. 'One with four legs, a tail and a very silly face.'

'Can he run fast?' Digby was tingling with excitement.

'I have to grant him that,' the cat said. 'He has the most extraordinary legs. Long black spindly things that seem to be made of elastic. But that's all he can do, run.'

'He's a greyhound, isn't he?' Digby cried. 'And I know him!'

The grey cat's eyes grew very round. 'How could you?' he queried. 'He's only been here a short while.'

Digby explained about the Dogs' Home. 'Is he here now? Can I see him?'

'No, you can't see him,' the cat replied stiffly. 'He's kept in a kennel round the back. Anyway, I thought you wanted to hide?'

'Yes,' Digby said, disappointed. 'Shall I bury myself among these plants?'

'That wasn't what I had in mind,' the grey cat told him. 'You'd soon be noticed there. Come this way.' He took Digby to the corner of the house where an open door led down to the cellar. Digby took one look, saw the yawning black gulf beneath him and backed swiftly away.

'What's the matter?' the cat asked, genuinely surprised. 'You're trembling all over.'

'I'm not going into another of those places. Is this some kind of trick?'

'Whatever are you talking about?' the cat hissed. 'How can it be a trick? I've never seen you before.'

'It's just like where the man tied me up,' Digby explained. 'I'm sorry. It makes me go all jangly. I didn't know what I was saying. I'll lie down here in the garden for a while until it's light.'

'Please yourself.' The cat was becoming bored.

'Will Streak come out?'

'Not on his own. He's not allowed,' the cat answered superciliously. 'He has to be shackled to a human before he can take a step.' His contempt for a dog on a lead knew no bounds.

Digby was weary. 'I don't believe it,' he muttered. 'If that's the case, how could you have seen him run?' He lay down. 'I'll wait for him,' he said.

9

After Digby had been whisked away in Green's car, Frank returned dejectedly to Keserly Street. Chip dogged his heels all the way, but his company was small consolation to the young man. To have come so close to rescuing Digby only to fail was the worst possible outcome. Frank knocked on Miss Crisp's door. She had his holdall ready. He quickly gave her the news and handed back her note.

'I shall distribute this,' the woman said. 'You never know; someone may have seen something.'

'You're very determined.' Frank looked sad. 'I'm afraid I've lost heart myself.'

From there he made his way to the hospital. Norman was recovering well and Frank wanted to tell him about Chip.

The old man was sitting up in bed and looking cheerful. His beard had been trimmed and his hair cut and combed. 'Frank, my dear boy,' he greeted his friend, 'you're a wonder.' Frank deposited Norman's radio by his bedside. 'I never dreamt you'd take this trouble over me.'

'I've found Chip,' Frank said. 'I thought you'd like to know.'

'Oh, that dog.' Norman chuckled. 'He can look after himself all right. He knows how to make out. Is he with you now?'

'Of course not. He's lurking in the car park. He follows me around. But we've no home, Norman. The squat's demolished.'

The old man took a moment to digest the news.

Then he said phlegmatically, 'It's a wonder it didn't happen before – it's been on the cards for years. So you're on the streets now?'

'What else? And Digby's been stolen.' He related the past events.

Norman listened to the tale but wasn't one to be put out. 'There's nothing more you can do,' he said. 'Don't waste your time fretting. And I'll take the other one off your hands when I get out of here.'

'What do you mean?' Frank asked in amazement. 'You're surely not going back to street life?'

Norman looked conspiratorial. He winked and leaned towards his visitor. 'Listen,' he whispered. 'They're trying to find me a place in a hostel. But they don't know me. I'm a singer.' He raised his voice and warbled a few bars of a popular song. 'I've been singing in here,' he resumed. 'I keep 'em all entertained. And I'll go on with it when I get out, whenever that is. I'm a singer and I sing for my supper.'

'You're too old to go back on the road,' Frank told him. 'You should be sensible. You've got used to a warm, dry bed and a bath.'

'Don't you worry about me, son,' Norman replied stubbornly. 'I've been a rover and a balladeer all my life. I've sung in bars all over the country. I'm too old to change. What about you, now? What plans have you with your life ahead of you?'

'I'm looking for a new squat,' Frank said. 'I'll keep Chip with me until you come out or until he tires of me. I've had some help, and there's some heavy labouring work going in the park. I'll try my luck there. And I'll keep busking.'

'Good boy,' Norman nodded. 'Keep in touch with me, or I won't know how to find you.'

They shook hands. Chip was waiting for Frank in the car park. The mongrel cocked his leg thoughtfully

against a Range Rover as he saw the young man appear.
Mr Perfect didn't seem quite so sure of himself these
days.

Digby skulked among the bushes in the garden for
what seemed an endless night. Occasionally he was able
to doze but the misery of hunger always nagged him
back to wakefulness. He longed to see Streak and he
greeted the daylight in a fever of impatience. There
was no sign of the grey cat and Digby wondered just
how secure he was where he lay half screened by plants,
waiting for the house to come to life. He was dying to
know how Streak had arrived at this place. And he felt
he could use the benefit of Streak's wisdom again.
    At last the front door opened and an elderly man
came out. Digby pressed himself against the ground.
The man walked slowly to the wrought-iron garden
gate, leading a grizzled black greyhound. As soon as
they were on the pavement and heading away from the
house, Digby leapt up. He squeezed a forepaw through
the gap underneath the other gate and tugged. Slowly
it yielded, and as soon as there was space enough Digby
dashed through. He pattered along behind the other
two. His hope was that Streak would eventually be
released to run free, enabling him to confront the
greyhound before the elderly human could prevent it.
But there seemed to be no possibility of its happening.
Streak was kept constantly under control. In a while
the greyhound sensed another dog behind him. He
turned his long head, saw Digby and stopped dead.
The elderly man urged Streak forward but the old
greyhound sat on his haunches, whining strangely. Now
Digby had no choice but to ran up.
    'Streak! is it you?' Digby yelped.
    'Yes, it's me, Bouncing Jet Streak of Fleetwood. Your
old pen pal!'

The dogs frolicked around one another in joy and excitement. The old man was so astonished to hear the quiet Streak barking that he took a while to recover himself.

'Stop! Stop it, Streak!' he ordered. He tried to shoo Digby away, assuming the collie was from a neighbour's house. 'Go away, go on. Go home,' he cried ineffectually. Digby ignored him.

'Where have you come from?' Streak whispered. 'Are you living nearby? Tell me quickly.'

'I'm lost,' Digby wailed plaintively. 'And I'm starving. I need help.' His choking voice made Streak's elderly owner realize something was amiss, and he bent down to lay a sympathetic hand on the collie's head. This simple act of human kindness was too much for Digby. Worn out by fear, ill-treatment, hunger and thirst he collapsed under the man's touch with an exhausted whimper.

'Dear dear me,' the old fellow murmured. 'Poor creature. There's something wrong here.' He could see there was no name tag on Digby's collar. 'I'd better see what I can do.' He released Streak to pick up the collie. 'Come on, Streak. You can have your walk later,' he said. 'This dog needs attention.'

On the short walk home Digby's stomach made itself heard in no uncertain manner. 'So that's it, is it?' the man pondered. 'He needs food. I wonder if that's all that's wrong with him? Well, we can soon put that right, anyway.'

Back in the house Digby was given milk and a plate of meat and biscuits. The smell of the food was sufficient to revive him and he made short work of it.

'What are we going to do with him?' the man's wife asked. 'That's no dog we know.'

'No indeed,' the old gentleman agreed. 'I think he

may be lost. Or abandoned,' he added as an after-
thought. 'One hears such things.'

'Should we ring the police?'

'I think so. But there's no rush. The poor animal
needs rest. We can put him outside with Streak. You
should have seen them together. Gambolling about like
a couple of puppies.'

While Streak's interrupted walk was resumed, Digby
was made comfortable in the greyhound's kennel. The
elderly lady watched him fall asleep with satisfaction.
While he slept the grey cat came to inspect him, not
at all pleased that Digby appeared to be permanently
lodged in his garden.

'This is too much,' he muttered. 'Is this a replace-
ment, or are we to have two dogs now?' But there was
no waking Digby and the collie was still fast asleep when
Streak returned. The greyhound lay down outside his
kennel, content to keep quiet until his friend was ready
to tell him what had happened. After a while Digby
stirred and sleepily opened one eye. When he saw
Streak's gentle face he let out a sigh of relief.

'It's wonderful to see you there,' he said. 'I feel so
much better.'

'That's good news,' said Streak. 'Are you up to telling
me your story?'

'I am. But first – how did *you* come here? Were you
chosen at last?'

'Yes. Even I've found a home,' Streak said happily.
'They're very kind people. I hope I'll see out my days
with them.'

'I'm so glad. Do you get on with the cat? He doesn't
seem to appreciate dogs.'

'Max? We tolerate each other. I don't let him bother
me. But how do you know about him?'

'I'd better start from the beginning,' Digby said. 'Oh,
Streak, how happy I am we've met again.'

Streak listened patiently and without interruption to Digby's tale. 'Poor friend, you've suffered badly,' he said afterwards. 'How unlucky can a dog be? You've twice lost your home and your master. But things will be better now. You'll see. They'll look after you here.'

Digby was doubtful. 'They didn't choose me, Streak. How do you know they'll want a second dog? Besides, I want to find my young master. He was very good to me.'

'Yes. I'm sure of it. Humans are very clever, aren't they, Digby? Perhaps my owners can find yours for you.'

They were trying to do exactly that. The old man had telephoned the police who confirmed that a dog answering the collie's description had been reported missing. As soon as they could arrange it, a police dog handler would call to collect the animal. The old man and his wife were delighted by the outcome and went outside to see how their visitor was coming along.

Digby's general air of contentment as he lay side by side with Streak told them all they wanted to know. The comradeship of the two dogs was heartwarming. 'It's as if they knew each other,' the old lady said wonderingly. Digby did indeed feel settled. But always at the back of his mind was the memory of his recent ordeal. The images of Ken and Green still loomed large.

In the afternoon the peacefulness of the garden was abruptly disturbed when the policeman arrived to take Digby away. Digby took one look at the burly uniformed figure and went into a panic. To him there was no distinction between the officer and the two sinister strangers who had captured and tormented him. The old couple could not quieten the collie, who chased hither and thither across the garden, terrified of being captured again.

'He hasn't been well. He's obviously frightened,' the old lady commented unnecessarily.

Streak attempted to calm Digby down with his gentle calls but the policeman raised objections. 'Perhaps you could remove your own dog, sir?' he suggested politely. 'I don't feel his barking can help the situation at all.'

The old man hastened to comply. But in the scramble Digby fled into the house along with Streak, then out of the open front door. It took no more than a few moments for the collie to tug the wooden gate ajar just as he had done before, and he was off down the street before anyone had realized what had happened.

The policeman jumped into his vehicle, hoping to keep the runaway in sight, but Digby veered off the main street as soon as he found an opportunity. He had the sense to realize he needed to get under cover. He pelted down a narrow lane only to find it led nowhere; a brick wall blocked off the end. There was a wide entrance on one side where two tall gates had been swung back. Digby ran through and found himself in a big yard where several hefty motor coaches were parked. Instinctively he aimed for one and crawled into the darkness underneath. The acrid smell of petrol and oil was overpowering, but Digby had no option but to remain where he was. He could see a pair of human legs moving across the yard and he was determined to stay hidden.

What Digby did not know was that he had preserved his liberty at a tremendous cost. By escaping the policeman he had sacrificed his chance of being reunited with his master.

10

Unknown to Digby, who only had flight on his mind, the old couple had hurried into the street to watch the policeman's efforts to catch him. They had temporarily forgotten Streak, who was able to sneak out behind them. The greyhound was really upset by Digby's sudden disappearance when they had only just found each other again. He stood in the garden, whining softly.

'Why don't you go after him?' Max purred from an outside window sill. The cat had seen everything. Streak looked up sharply. Max had guessed his thoughts. 'Quickly,' he urged. 'You haven't much time. You're not much good at anything else but you *have* got speed.'

Streak stepped quietly through the open garden gate. His owners had their backs to him as they craned their necks in Digby's direction. Without hesitating any longer the greyhound launched himself forward, shot past the elderly couple and set his sights on the blur of movement that Digby had become in the distance.

The speed of the racing dog was, even now, some-thing to marvel at. Streak's long legs simply devoured the long street ahead. People stopped to gaze in wonder and curiosity, but he cared nothing for that. He glimpsed Digby turning into the lane and pelted after him. By the time Streak had also turned the corner, however, Digby had vanished into the coach yard. Streak slackened his pace, looking round for his friend. The policeman's car had passed the turning and Streak was free to explore as he wished.

A coach turned into the lane and lumbered towards

the yard, its engine droning noisily. Streak watched
where it went, and realized that Digby must have
hidden himself somewhere in that yard. There was
nowhere else he could have gone. He trotted forward
cautiously. The coach came to a halt, and the driver
climbed out and spoke to another man who was
carrying a clipboard. Streak peered round the side of
the gate, keeping his body out of sight. There was no
sign of Digby. Streak didn't venture into the yard while
the men were close. Eventually they strolled towards a
small office and went inside.

'Digby! Are you there?' Streak called quietly.

No answer.

Streak waited a little to ensure that the men were
still safely out of hearing. Then he called more loudly.
'Digby! Digby! Can you hear me? It's Streak.'

This time there was a muffled response, almost
inaudible thanks to the huge mass of the coach frame-
work above him. But Streak caught something of it and
inched further into the yard.

'Where are you?'

'Underneath,' Digby barked, rather unhelpfully.

This time the men heard. They came out of the
office and glanced round. Digby stayed hidden, but
the men soon spotted Streak by the entrance. The yard
manager went towards him, waving his arms to drive
him away. Streak retreated into the lane and sat down
a metre or so away. The man shouted at him and, with
the assistance of the coach driver, swung the heavy
gates closed. There were no more vehicles due in and
the yard was made secure with bolts and padlocks.

Streak hung about outside, fretting with vexation.
There was no other way in, but he wasn't going to
desert Digby. He remained just out of reach, in case
the men decided to come after him, but he need not
have worried. Once the yard gates were shut the men

forgot all about him. Some while later a little door opened in the wall of the yard and the coach driver stepped out and walked to a parked car nearby. Streak watched this narrow opening tensely. Should he try to slip through it or should he alert Digby to this slim chance of escape? He edged towards it, unsure what to do and fearful in case the other man should suddenly appear. The coach driver left, his car disappearing into the main street. Streak felt he must at least try to contact Digby. He reached the open door just as the yard manager was locking his office, and realized he was too late to join his friend.

'Digby, here! Run! Run quickly!' he barked as loudly as he could.

Digby began to scramble from under the parked coach. But as he was about to pull himself clear he saw the yard manager striding towards the door in the wall, and he shrank back again. Streak barked even more urgently.

'Now, Digby! Run before it's too late!'

The man ran towards the greyhound, shouting at him angrily. He knew nothing about the collie's presence and saw Streak only as a noisy nuisance. Streak could see Digby's one chance was lost and made haste to retreat from the angry human. Moments later the man stood in the lane with the little door closed behind him. Digby was alone in the yard with no way out.

Streak kept his distance until the manager had also driven away. Then he crept back and positioned himself by the high yard gates. Digby's frightened whines could be heard on the other side.

'Calm down. Calm down, Digby,' Streak called to him. 'There's nothing to be done now. We shall have to be patient.'

Digby could hear Streak clearly through the chinks in the gates. Relief flooded over him as he realized the greyhound was still nearby. 'Streak, you're such a friend! But what about your owners? They'll be missing you terribly.'

'I know,' the greyhound answered soberly. 'That can't be helped. I know where they are and I can go back when I choose.'

'Are you sure? Won't they be searching for you?'

'That's a danger I'll have to face. But they're not very quick and, if necessary, I could easily evade them.'

'Why would you want to? Because of me?' Digby's voice was hushed.

'Yes. I'll stay around here until you can get away. Then we must keep together. We haven't discovered each other again to be parted so soon.'

'I'm so grateful to you,' Digby said feelingly. 'Your company makes all this bearable. But I don't want to be the means of separating you from your kind owners.'

'We'll see it through, you and I,' Streak assured him. 'It may not take too long.'

Digby wasn't absolutely sure he understood. 'See what through, Streak?'

'Why, restoring you to your master, of course. Whatever else?'

'Well, of course that's what I want,' Digby said. 'But I don't know where he is any more.'

'There must be ways of finding him. We have noses,' Streak pointed out. 'Another thing – we have to eat. Have you any ideas on that score?'

'There's nothing to eat in here.'

'I know that, Digby. I wasn't talking about what's behind this barrier. I mean, once we're together.'

'Oh. No, I've no ideas at all. I've never had to feed myself. Have you?'

'No. But I'm confident we can. We just have to find out how.'

'Bouncing Jet Streak of Fleetwood,' Digby murmured, savouring the sound. 'You know, you really deserve a special name like that.'

Streak kept his gaze along the length of the lane. He knew it was only a matter of time before one, at least, of his owners showed up. 'Listen, Digby,' he said, 'I'm going to move now. If someone comes after me here I haven't anywhere to run to. I'll make myself scarce until it gets dark. Then I'll come back.'

Digby knew it made sense but he hated the idea of being left alone again. 'You're sure you'll come back?' he asked nervously.

'It's a promise,' Streak answered. He ran up the lane, and stopped dead. His owner, the old man, was in sight further down the main street. Evidently it hadn't yet occurred to him to search any of the minor turnings off it. Streak ran in the opposite direction, back towards his home. He knew the perfect place to hide – the cellar below his own garden.

He made certain that his mistress wasn't on the look-out and then leapt athletically over the low garden fence. Max was in the front garden and Streak almost landed on top of him.

'Clumsy dog,' the cat complained. 'You could have flattened me!'

'Never mind that. Is the mistress indoors?'

'Probably. She usually is, isn't she? And where's your friend? Didn't you find him?'

'Oh yes, I found him,' Streak replied. 'He'll be all right where he is for now. And *I'm* going down here,' he told the cat as he entered the dark cellar. 'Don't let on by calling outside or leading one of the dear humans in to me,' he cautioned Max. 'It would spoil everything and you wouldn't want that.'

Max recognized the veiled threat but pretended not to notice. 'You've no worries on my account,' he mewed. 'I don't involve myself in dogs' concerns.'

In their different hiding places Digby and Streak were both acutely aware of their stomachs' demands. Digby, in particular, had eaten only one substantial meal in a number of days. Both of them thought almost exclusively about food. Streak racked his brains for a solution to the problem of feeding, while Digby was reminded of Chip.

'He lived on the streets,' he thought to himself. 'How did *he* manage?'

By the time it was dark Streak had heard movements and voices overhead which told him that both the old lady and her husband were back in the house. He emerged tentatively from the cellar. All was well. He set off on the return journey.

Digby was already by the yard gates, listening for his friend. 'I'm so glad you're here,' he said when Streak trotted up. 'What can we do about eating? I'm half starved.'

'Nothing for the present,' Streak answered. 'We've got to get you out of there first.'

'There's no way out,' Digby sighed. 'I've looked all round.'

'The men will be back, never fear,' Streak assured him. 'As soon as they make an opening you must run for it.'

'You bet I will,' Digby said. 'I don't know why I thought they meant me any harm.'

'You got yourself all jangly.'

They settled down as best they could for the night on either side of the gates, their empty stomachs rumbling in sympathy with one another. In the morning, sure enough, the yard manager arrived. Streak moved away from the gates, but not before he was spotted. The man stared at him, but this time did no more than shake his head. Then he went to the little door and unlocked it. As soon as it was open, Digby came rushing

up and darted through before the manager had a
chance to enter. The man turned quickly and saw greyhound and collie running together up the lane.

'So *that's* what he was hanging around for,' he mar-
velled.

'Where to now?' Digby asked. The main street was still
fairly empty.

'I don't know. We need to make for the area where
your master is likely to be if we're going to look for
him. Which way is that?'

'I've no idea,' Digby confessed. 'I told you; I was
brought here in a car.'

'Of course. Then we'll just have to do the best we
can.' Streak replied. 'I know a lot of the roads round
here. I'll take you to the quietest part.'

'Shall we look for food on the way?'

'Certainly. There must be scraps around if I know
human habits. We'll keep our noses active and see how
we get on.'

11

Frank tried to forget about Digby but it was impossible to erase the young border collie's image from his mind. He decided to do something positive, and applied for the job in the park. The supervisor gave him a curious look.

'I know you, don't I?' he asked. 'Anyway, I've seen you around.'

'Maybe. Does that stand against me?'

'No, not necessarily. What experience have you got of this kind of work?'

'None especially. Only the strength I was born with, which might just be sufficient for a labouring job.'

'Are you being sarcastic?' the supervisor asked suspiciously.

'I didn't mean to be, no.'

'All right. I'll tell you about the work and then I'll need to ask some more questions.'

At the end of the interview, Frank was taken on at once on a provisional basis to see how he coped. The supervisor held the door open as Frank left.

'Is that your dog sitting there waiting?' he asked. Chip was doing just that.

'Not exactly mine, no,' Frank replied.

'Because you'll have to leave him behind if he is. We don't allow staff to bring pets into the park.'

'Understood,' Frank answered. 'I'll see he goes home before I start.'

'Be quick about it, then.'

Here was a problem. There was no home for Chip to go to and Frank wasn't at all optimistic about his ability to drive the mongrel out of the park and make him stay away. Chip had got too used to Frank's good nature and relied on him more and more.

'Now, Chip.' The dog was looking at him expectantly. 'I need this job. I can't earn enough busking and I want a place of my own. Doorways aren't comfortable and I've been used to just a little more luxury. So you're going to have to leave me – at least until later. This job could be my passport to a proper home – and proper food for both of us. Come on, then.' He led Chip a few steps and then pointed to the nearby street. 'Go and find Norman. Go. That way!' He raised his voice to one of command, gesturing firmly that Chip must leave him. The mongrel trotted a little way off, then turned to see if Frank was following. When he saw that he wasn't, he began to run back.

'No!' Frank cried. 'No! Go back! Oh, Chip,' he muttered beneath his breath, 'don't muck this up for me.' He ran towards Chip, shouting at him to go. In the end Chip took the hint and ran off with a puzzled and rather hurt expression on his face.

Frank went to see the head gardener and receive his instructions. He felt sad and guilty and Chip's bewildered look stayed in his mind. He would go on feeding the mongrel if Chip stayed in the locality, but any care or attention could only be given after working hours.

He was put to work on a rockery which was being constructed in a corner of the park. His job consisted mainly of humping huge chunks of sandstone from one place to another and setting them in position. Even with a wheelbarrow it was heavy going. While he was busy Frank kept wondering how he could make Chip understand that he must keep out of sight until he was called at the end of the day. He knew Chip was intelligent, but this was a tall order and Frank didn't think the dog could manage it. He didn't expect to find Chip again.

Frank's reckoning proved to be wrong. Chip hadn't

given up on him. After the initial shock, the mongrel gradually crept back towards the park entrance. Of course by then Frank was working in quite another quarter, but that didn't bother Chip, who knew the park well. Wary as ever, he kept away from the main paths and used the ground cover to screen his movements as much as he could. He needed to know why Frank had behaved as he had done. He didn't yet believe that they could no longer be friends.

Frank eventually saw Chip at a distance, his head up, sniffing the air with one front paw raised. It was clear that he had caught Frank's scent and was now starting forward uncertainly.

'Oh no,' Frank moaned to himself. 'What can I do?'

Chip trotted nearer, saw Frank, paused irresolutely and waved his tail in recognition.

'That your dog?' another gardener asked. 'He seems to know you.'

'No, he's *not* my dog,' Frank answered with irritation. 'He – he keeps following me around. I suppose I was too friendly to him once and now he's a bit of a nuisance.'

'Well, I wouldn't be friendly any more if I were you. They don't like stray dogs running about here and it could get you into trouble.'

'I know. I've already been warned about it,' Frank said. He continued with his work, deciding his best policy was to ignore Chip altogether.

The dog came no closer. Receiving no encouragement, he remained in a state of uncertainty. He skulked around among some bushes where he could still watch Frank without too many people being aware of it.

At the end of the day, sore and aching from his labours, Frank helped return the tools to the store. His workmates left for home in dribs and drabs. Frank stayed on, seated himself on one of the rockery slabs and played his mouth-organ. He didn't want to be seen leaving in case Chip followed him. When he was sure he was on his own he picked up the holdall with all his belongings in it and walked off slowly.

'I carry my home with me,' he thought. 'I must find a different place to sleep tonight. If I were discovered by any of the park staff I'd be out straight away.' The supervisor had been more than lenient with him already, but Frank knew he was suspicious. Frank had had none of the necessary documents required by an employer, and had the labouring job been a permanent one he'd never have been offered it.

'If I can just stay on here long enough to get myself a room somewhere,' he mused. 'There are no squats to be had round these parts any more.'

Chip emerged from the shrubbery and bounded up hopefully. Frank wasn't hard-hearted enough to resist him. 'All right, Chip,' he said. 'I know you don't understand what's going on. We can stay together for now. You must be famished.'

After filling their stomachs Frank and Chip settled down under a railway arch near the river. 'Tomorrow,' said the young man to the dog, 'I'm going to have to teach you a whole new meaning of the word "stay".' Frank fell asleep, thinking of Digby.

The next morning Frank awoke at dawn feeling dreadfully stiff. Every muscle in his body seemed to ache and his hands had been scratched by the rough stones of the new rockery. 'Worth it in the long run,' he whispered to himself.

Chip stirred and stretched his limbs.

'You'd do better to stay here,' Frank told him. 'But I know you won't.'

When he arrived, hobbling, at the park entrance, he managed to make Chip understand that he was to come no further. Chip put his head on one side and watched

Frank walk on, believing he would be back in a short while. It never occurred to him that he was supposed to stay there all day.

When they saw him, Frank's workmates chuckled at his awkward movements.

'The first week's the worst,' one of them laughed. 'Then you should get used to it.'

The rockery was beginning to look really impressive. Frank was quite proud of his part in it. When the other men strolled off to eat their sandwiches at midday he stayed on, doing a little unpaid labour as he resettled some of the rocks in a more natural way. He had no lunch to eat and he was determined to keep his back to the spot where Chip had skulked the previous day. Frank guessed the mongrel was probably lurking in the shrubbery again.

A voice behind him startled him. It was not the voice of any of his fellow workers; it was rather too cultured. 'You've made a wonderful start on that.'

Frank turned and saw a man in late middle age, shortish and tubby, dressed in a suit, with a broad smile on his face.

'It's not all my effort,' Frank answered honestly, grinning back. 'But thanks.'

'Hard work, I should think.'

'Yes.' Frank pulled a face. 'I'm all aches today. But I'm not too bothered. Having a job's the main thing.'

'Absolutely.' The older man nodded. 'You look as if the outdoor life suits you. You have a good colour. You must have been doing this sort of thing for quite a while?'

Frank thought quickly. He knew only too well where his colour came from. But he didn't want to give the slightest indication of his homeless state. He didn't know who this man was. 'Oh well, you know,' he said vaguely. 'I forget exactly.'

'Mmm.' The man stepped closer. 'Actually,' he said, lowering his voice, 'I'm looking for someone to help out in my garden. If you know of anyone who might be interested, I'd be glad to hear from them. It'd be a full-time job. There's an awful lot to do. My wife and I can't cope with it. We've only been in the house a short while. The previous owner rather let the garden go.'

'A full-time job?' Frank repeated, trying to hide his excitement.

'Yes. And there would be accommodation to go with it. There's a sort of cabin in the grounds – very tiny but big enough for an unattached young man.'

Frank gaped. This was too good to be true.

The man could see he had caught the bait. 'Would you know of anybody? Here's my card. There's the number to ring. Hello – is this your dog?'

Chip had turned up, wagging his tail, and eager to see who Frank was talking to.

'We couldn't take anyone with a dog,' the man said firmly. 'We have one of our own. It wouldn't work. Matter of fact, we had two of our own at one time, but what with the house move and everything else to deal with we had to get rid of one of them.'

'It's not my dog,' Frank said in what he hoped was a convincing tone. 'It's a stray that comes round here looking for titbits.' He raised his voice and said as firmly as he could, 'I wish it would *leave me alone.*'

'I see.' The other man turned to go. 'Well, you have my card. Perhaps you can talk to your mates; see if anyone's interested. Mustn't hold you up any more. Nice talking to you.' He strode away, leaving Frank clutching the business card and glaring at Chip. For a moment, all he could see was a potential obstacle between himself and a full-time job (with accommodation!). This was the best chance to come his way since his father had thrown him out.

'Go away!' Frank shouted at the dog. '*Go away!*'

Chip stopped cavorting about and looked nervously

at Mr Perfect. The new harsh tone in the man's voice
added to the dog's previous uncertainties. Chip's tail
drooped and he backed a few steps, then turned and
ran off with a frightened little yelp. Frank slumped
down on one of the small boulders, feeling thoroughly
miserable. After a while he pulled out his mouth-organ
and blew at it guiltily.

The tune calmed him but he didn't dare look round
to see where Chip was, so he played on. The plaintive
music carried a little distance, and someone stepped
slowly towards Frank to listen. He waited until the tune
was ended before he spoke.

'*That's* where I know you from!' he exclaimed. 'You
used to play by the underground station. You had a
dog with you.'

Frank looked up sharply. The staff manager who had
given him his job was staring at him.

'You're homeless, aren't you?'

Frank nodded wretchedly.

'Yes. Well, I'm afraid this puts a different complexion
on things,' the manager remarked, not unsympathetic-
ally. 'I don't think I—'

'You don't have to say it,' Frank interrupted him. 'I'll
leave. Will you pay me for the work I've done?'

'Of course. Come to my office in the morning and
we'll settle up. I'm sorry, but I'm sure you understand
that in a public position . . . I'd be happy to put in a
word for you privately, though, if it would help. You're
a good worker.'

Frank pocketed his mouth-organ. His hand touched
the business card he had been given a little earlier, and
his spirits lifted a trifle.

At the park gate a keeper recognized Chip and grasped
him. Later that evening the Dogs' Home received a
new admission.

12

Meanwhile, Digby and Streak were acting like two strays themselves. Neither of them, however, had Chip's instinct for survival on the streets. The older dog took the lead and Digby was happy to let him. They made their way first to some public gardens that Streak knew well as a quiet refuge from traffic and noise. There was a pond in the centre, and Digby had a long drink. A small café stood next to the pond, and Streak knew where they could find scraps from the kitchen. The two dogs slunk around the containers of rubbish at the back of the café, pulling and tearing at bags and cartons. They found very little to their liking.

'We're not cut out for this kind of thing,' Digby said. 'We've always been used to better rations.'

'Beggars can't be choosers,' Streak reminded him. 'We have to eat what and where we can until you're settled again.'

'Streak, you don't have to do this,' Digby said guiltily. 'You have a good home. Please go back. Why should you suffer because of me?'

'Because I choose to,' Streak replied quietly. 'Don't worry on my account. I can bear this for a bit. Let's make sure it *is* only for a bit, though. How can we pick up the right trail? Can you think of any clue that would help?'

Digby swallowed a lump of stale bread and thought hard. 'Would you know the way to the compound from here?' he asked.

'Compound? You mean the Dogs' Home?'

'Yes. If you could get us there I'd know what to do. I remember everything about the day I was chosen.'

'All right,' said Streak. 'I'll try my best. I think I know how we should go. It'll be the opposite way from my way home. We'll just keep running.'

'But, Streak,' Digby begged, 'don't run at your usual pace. I won't be able to keep up!'

Frank left the park without a backward glance. He carried his holdall in his left hand; with his right he continually fingered the card in his pocket. He couldn't decide whether to get in touch. It all seemed too perfect. Life didn't work like that: one day you were homeless and penniless and the next set up in a job with a home included. At least, not in his experience. But then again, why not? Stranger things had happened. Maybe this was the turning point. He walked aimlessly along with no definite direction in mind. His head was full of dreams. If he *could* get this job, if he could stay in it, if he could have his own little place . . . well, the past with all its unpleasantness and trials could be forgotten. He could even write to his father and stepmother and tell them where he was. They hadn't been in touch for many years.

He took the card out and read it for the twentieth time.

James Odling
Rothesay House
29 Berwyn Road
Tel. 0171–876 2226

There was a telephone box along the road. Frank thought it too soon to make the call. He bought himself some fish and chips and ate them from the paper, seated on the kerb. Afterwards he sat looking at the telephone box and watched people making their calls.

He told himself he'd count up to a dozen and then, after the twelfth person had used the telephone, he would use it himself. If he struck lucky with thirteen, then he really would believe that the whole thing wasn't a hoax.

More than an hour had passed by the time the twelfth person had finished telephoning. Frank hauled himself to his feet and winced at his aching limbs. He stepped to the box and, without any further hesitation, dialled Mr Odling's number. A young girl answered, and Frank asked for her father.

'James Odling.' Frank recognized the voice.

'Good afternoon. We spoke earlier about a gardening job.' Frank's heart pounded excitedly. 'I have your card.'

'Ah yes. Well, you're very prompt. Are you interested yourself, or is there someone—'

'No, no, it's me. I want the job. I mean, I would like to take the job if it's offered,' Frank babbled. He closed his eyes, clenching the phone tightly as he waited for the reply.

'Fine. Come and see us. You might change your mind when you see the garden.' Odling laughed.

'Oh no. No. I won't,' Frank assured him.

'OK. Can you come this evening? Good. About six? Right then. Here are the directions . . .'

Frank scrabbled for a pen and quickly noted down what he was told on the back of the business card. He came out of the telephone box chanting 'Lucky thirteen, lucky thirteen' to the amusement of a passer-by of whom Frank then asked the time.

'Four fifteen.'

He hadn't long. 'I must make myself respectable,' he said to himself. He quickly calculated his loose change. There was just enough to buy a five-pound shirt from a bargain clothes market he knew. Was there time?

'There'll have to be,' he decided, and began to run.
The holdall slowed him down but he did the best he
could. In the market he snatched the first shirt of
suitable size. Then into a busy pub while the barman
wasn't looking to make use of its facilities to change
and wash. Five o'clock.

'The jeans will have to stay. But he's seen them
already so I've nothing to lose there.' His hair was too
long, he had a slight beard, his jacket was worn, his
shoes were scuffed . . . 'Lucky thirteen, lucky thirteen,'
he chanted as he tried to tidy himself.

The new shirt scratched his skin. He stuffed his old
one in his bag and dashed from the building. It had
started to rain. He glanced at his directions and set off
at an uneven trot.

By the time he reached Rothesay House Frank was
very wet. Water dripped from his hair and ran down
his face and neck on to his clean shirt. Still, there was
nothing he could do about the weather. He took a
towel out of his bag and dried his head a little while
he looked at the premises.

The house was a large Edwardian building with three
steps leading up to an elaborate porch. There were a
lot of windows and an imposing front door. But it was
the front garden which mostly occupied Frank's gaze.
It consisted of a lawn around which was a gravel drive
and a collection of tremendously overgrown shrubs. All
the plants seemed to be growing into each other. The
immediate impression was one of gloom; almost fore-
boding. Frank whistled. 'Lucky thirteen,' he muttered.
He raked his fingers through his hair and hurried to
the front door.

Odling answered his knock. 'You're late,' he
remarked irritably as soon as he saw the young man.

'Am I? I'm really sorry. I don't have a watch and I
thought I was in good time,' Frank apologized.

'It's ten past six,' Odling announced.

Frank gulped. Was the man always going to be so precise?

'You'd better come through,' Odling said. 'What's that you have there? Your luggage? This is rather premature, isn't it? You won't be staying tonight, you know.'

Frank thought quickly. 'It's just some things I picked up from work,' he invented.

Odling took no notice. He led Frank through the lofty hall and via the kitchen to the back garden. His wife and daughter followed them out. Frank's jaw dropped as he saw the size of the wilderness before him. It was apparent that, apart from mowing the long rectangular lawn, no one had done anything to the garden for an age.

'You see our problem?' Odling commented.

'I do indeed,' Frank admitted. 'It would be difficult to know where to start.'

'Changed your mind?'

'Well – er – no. But it would take months of work to get it into any semblance of shape.'

'Exactly. That's why we don't want an ordinary jobbing gardener. Our aim is to enjoy our garden and a keen young man like you should regard that aim as a challenge.' Odling fixed his eyes intently on Frank. 'Otherwise you'll be no use to us.'

'I appreciate that,' said Frank.

'Come, I'll show you the shack. That's what my daughter calls it.'

Frank followed him to a corner of the garden which was slightly less unkempt than the rest. Among some tall rhododendrons, in a sort of clearing, stood a wooden summerhouse, amply proportioned and in good condition. Odling unlocked the door. It was neat and tidy inside. There was a sitting area, a small kitchenette with cooker and fridge and a tiny bathroom. At the other end stood a divan bed.

'All mod. cons,' Odling joked. 'You've got light, heat, running water. The previous owner made it into a kind of granny flat.'

Frank was delighted. The shack was light and airy. 'It's wonderful,' he said.

'I thought I might do my homework in here sometimes,' Odling's daughter told him. She was tall and dark and about twelve years of age, Frank guessed. 'Mummy and Daddy don't like my music.'

'I hope you won't mind if I borrow it?' he asked kindly.

The girl smiled. 'No. It'll be used properly again.'

'We've got all the tools you'll need. All you have to do is supply the muscle and diligence,' Odling said. 'Judging by the new rockery in the park you could make a good show here too.'

Frank forbore from repeating his denial that the rockery work had all been his. 'I'd do my very best,' he said simply.

'Well now, how much notice do you have to give?'

'None. I'm paid on a daily basis,' Frank fibbed.

'Oh really?' Odling looked at him for a few moments as though undecided. Then he turned and locked the summer house. 'Well, here you'd be on a weekly arrangement. As we don't know each other, I'd have to start you on no more than eighty. Then we'll see how we go on. Of course all your power and water would be paid for. How does that sound?'

Frank thought of cold pavements, draughty squats and busking. 'It sounds like a dream,' he murmured before he could stop himself.

'A what?' Odling asked sharply.

'Nothing. I mean – um – well, it's just fine,' Frank assured him.

'Good, good. Well, I'll have a word with the park supervisor, and if he's happy with you let's say you'll start the day after tomorrow. We'll sort out all the paperwork when you arrive. Let's go indoors now before we all end up soaked.'

A dog began to bark from a back room as Frank re-entered the house. He remembered Odling's regulation, and felt a mixture of guilt and relief that Chip appeared to have given up on him. The man shook hands with him and the wife and daughter looked pleased. The young man's pleasant, unassuming manner and his pleasing accent had won them over at once. Frank left the house, shut the garden gate and said to himself for the umpteenth time, 'Lucky thirteen. The day after tomorrow *is* the thirteenth. So this really does look like Fate.'

However, until that date, Frank still had two more nights of discomfort to endure. He decided to use the shelter of the railway arch again. As he rushed along through the rain he could barely contain his excitement. It was difficult to credit what had happened, his luck had changed so suddenly. He still felt guilty about the way he had banished Chip but tried to comfort himself with the thought that the mongrel had never really been his.

Safely ensconced under the arch, Frank was very wet but he felt no discomfort. In his mind he was already living in the wooden cabin in the garden of Rothesay House. He daydreamed about how he would arrange the place to his satisfaction and then chuckled to himself. 'I've nothing to arrange,' he thought. 'I must buy some things with the money I'll get tomorrow.'

After an hour or so the dampness of his clothing began to irk him. He repacked his bag abruptly and walked to a nearby pizza restaurant. Over a mug of coffee he gradually dried out. The last thing he wanted now was to catch a bad chill.

He slept well, dry and warm for the most part. In the morning he had a hasty wash and then returned to the park to collect his wages. The sun was shining and pockets of mist rose from the saturated grass and leaves. Everything smelt fresh and new and Frank experienced a wonderful feeling of well-being.

The staff manager paid out what was owed almost without a word. Then, as Frank was leaving, the man said, 'I had a phone call from a Mr Odling half an hour ago. He wanted a reference, so I told him the reason you were leaving here was nothing that would stop you being an excellent employee anywhere else. Has he offered you a job?'

'Yes, he has.'

'Gardening work?'

'Yes.' Frank smiled. 'Of another kind. Working in a wilderness.' He left the manager, whistling happily. Not until he reached the park gate did he count his money over and plan what to do with it. There were several things he needed to buy – a razor, for instance – but chiefly he needed clothes. But first there was a small debt to settle.

He strode towards Keserly Street. It was a glorious day and he felt he wanted to share it with somebody. He was disappointed to find there was no answer at Miss Crisp's flat. Frank folded a ten-pound note into a scrap of paper and wrote a short message on the outside. Then he pushed it through the woman's letterbox. He was still longing to tell someone about his good luck, and suddenly he thought of Norman. He wasn't sure if he was still in hospital, but decided he would try.

He found the old man sitting in an easy chair in the

television room. Despite his bandages he looked very comfortable.

'My only visitor!' he exclaimed as Frank walked in. 'You've certainly been faithful to me.'

Frank grinned. 'You're going to find adjusting to the outside again very difficult,' he observed.

'Don't you worry about me,' Norman answered, shaking his head. 'I told you that before. What's your news?'

Frank described everything that had happened, including his rejection of Chip.

Norman looked pensive. 'I'm very glad for you,' he said. 'But I wish the dog could have been spared that.'

'I'm sorry,' Frank said miserably. 'You can see how it was. I – I *had* to, Norman.'

'Yes. All right, my boy. D'you think the scamp will come looking for me when I'm out of here?'

'He'll be around. You know Chip. He'll survive.'

Norman nodded. 'Yes. We'll find each other. You did what you could for him, and I'm grateful. You're not to feel bad about losing him. I'd have done the same, I'm sure.'

Frank didn't linger. He had some purchases to make. 'I'll look out for you,' he told Norman. 'Take care of yourself.'

Towards the end of the day Frank found himself wandering into the park. He was curious to see how the rockery was developing. The place was deserted. He sat down on a boulder and took out his mouth-organ. Miss Crisp's holdall was by his side. 'I won't be carrying you around much longer, like a snail with its shell,' he said to it. 'Tomorrow I'll be in my new home.' And he launched into a jaunty tune to celebrate.

13

Digby and Streak were making slow progress. Digby hadn't yet completely recovered from his ordeal and tired quickly. It was in the greyhound's nature to run at speed and he found it difficult to adjust his pace to the other dog's requirements. The food they managed to pick up didn't help Digby's return to health. It was meagre and irregular. But as they continued along first Streak, and then Digby, began to recognize certain features of the townscape.

'I wish I could go faster,' Digby sighed as they paused for a rest behind a bus shelter. He could think of nothing except Frank's gentle voice and shining face. 'I shall be so excited when we finally see each other!' He flopped down, quite exhausted.

'We should eat something,' Streak said. 'My stomach's growling at me again. And it's raining. We need shelter.'

'You're very sensible, aren't you?' Digby murmured. 'You never lose your dignity.'

Streak was amused. 'It's not dignity,' he answered, 'only old age.'

When Digby was ready they moved on. Streak had found nothing edible in the bus shelter but as they neared another street, a busier one, they both caught the smell of cooked meat. They trotted forward eagerly, noses working at a great rate. Digby was so occupied with locating the source of the delicious scent that he didn't immediately take note of the place they had reached. It was the same street where the horrible Ken had grabbed him. A youth was squatting in a doorway, munching a beefburger, a bag of hot food at his side. The two dogs, overcome by hunger, approached closer, licking their chops and looking at the youngster for the slightest sign of sympathy. There was none.

'Clear off!' he shouted. 'Ken! Two dogs here!'

The big man suddenly appeared from another doorway. Digby and Streak, frightened by the boy's shouts, actually ran in the most dangerous direction: towards Ken. The man had no idea that Digby was the dog he had captured earlier. He had no reason to suspect. He had been paid for his work and had forgotten about it. But Digby remembered at once. As soon as he smelt the man he barked in fright and at the same moment Ken lunged for him, catching him by one leg. Digby struggled to free himself, terrified of the torment he had only just managed to escape.

'Come and help, Denis,' Ken roared to the young man. 'I don't think I can hold him. Ow!' The man cried out as Streak's teeth sank into his other arm. He let go of Digby, who raced off in such terror that he forgot all about his friend. Denis and Ken between them wrestled Streak to the ground. The greyhound was too old to be of any use as a means of making money, but Ken intended to punish him for the hurt he had inflicted. Streak began to yap in alarm and distress. It was such an unexpected sound that Digby skidded to a halt and looked round. Never had he heard Streak bark like that before. He hesitated. The impulse to flee was still uppermost. But a cry of real pain from Streak made his own fright vanish, to be replaced by a bitter hatred. Barking loudly himself, Digby rushed back to the scene and snapped at the two vicious humans in a fury.

'Look out!' Ken cried. 'It might be rabid!'

That last word was sufficient to secure Streak's release. Denis let go of the greyhound and leapt away at the same time as Ken unfastened his grip. Streak was on his feet in a second and the two dogs galloped off through the relentless rain.

Streak had received a real shock. He had never been struck by a human before and the blow delivered by Ken had really unnerved him. Oblivious of his surroundings, weather, hunger or companionship, he bounded forward on his long legs. Digby was left far behind, and eventually the collie gave up the chase. He accepted that they were now separated. After a while he slowed down and finally stopped running altogether. He knew where he was: the park where he had met Chip lay before him. He lay down, panting heavily, under a thick bush. Raindrops cascaded through the leaves but Digby was too tired to care. He soon fell asleep.

Later in the night, Digby woke, roused by an all-pervading hunger. He left his shelter, shook his coat vigorously and began to search for scraps. He found some bread crusts someone had dropped for the birds and, soggy though they were, he wolfed them down in a twinkling. He wandered here and there, his nose working hard to pick up the faintest scent of food. He came to the spot where Frank's workmates had eaten their lunches. There were various bits and pieces in a litter bin which was easily turned over, but he found nothing at all satisfying. However, Digby's unappeased hunger was forgotten as he detected, albeit faintly, a more familiar scent. With mounting excitement he snuffled the air, then bent his nose to the ground. The heavy rain hadn't quite obscured all trace of Frank.

'*Now* I'll find him,' Digby barked in sheer joy. Without a further thought about eating he bent his muzzle to the trail. As he followed its broken course back to the park gate, it grew light. It promised to be a splendid day. Outside the park, however, the wet pavements, trodden by so many more pairs of feet, yielded no trace of Frank. Digby didn't lose heart. He thought he knew the way to their old home, but when he reached Keserly Street, early in the morning, he saw only the vacant plot where the squat had once stood. There was no sign of Frank. In fact, at that moment, the young man was collecting his wages from the staff manager in the park Digby had just left; man and dog had missed each other by minutes.

Digby wondered where he should go next. He wished Streak were still with him. He felt that the greyhound would have had some ideas. 'But I mustn't be selfish,' he thought to himself. 'I hope Streak is back with his master by now.' Digby trotted off down the road, expecting Chip to suddenly show up and guide him. As the day wore on he realized he was truly on his own and must rely entirely on himself.

By early evening Digby's anxiety was at its height. He was at his wits' end. Frank had eluded him all day. A discarded sandwich had been his only meal and now he was very weary. He remembered that Frank's scent had been strongest in the park and, since it still seemed to be his best hope, he headed once more in that direction.

As Digby neared the entrance his ears picked up a well-loved sound. Frank was sitting by the rockery, blowing a lively tune in solitude. Digby stopped, lifted up his head and howled. A park keeper peered round the corner of his hut, saw the unaccompanied collie and quickly moved towards him, but Digby had had quite enough of human interference. He dodged the keeper expertly and ran into the park, already beginning to bark an exultant welcome. As Frank continued to play his music, lost in his dreams of the wilderness, Digby burst through the shrubbery and leapt on top of him, whimpering with relief and licking his face, hands, neck and everything else he could reach in a kind of frenzy.

Frank dropped his mouth-organ. 'Digby! Oh, Digby! It's all right, it's all right!' He hugged his dog and tears sprang to his eyes. The park keeper arrived, saw the joy of the man and his dog, and left them with a smile and a wave.

'Oh, Digby, however did you escape?' Frank cried. 'You clever dog! I thought we were parted for ever. And now – what are we going to do?'

Digby spun round blissfully, his happy face showing exactly what he thought they were going to do: stay together for ever. Frank came down to earth first.

'But you're so thin, you poor old chap,' he said. 'Has someone been starving you? I shall never know what you've been through.' He tried to put the thought aside. 'Come on, you need feeding. And I've the money now for a feast.' He slung his holdall over his arm. Digby whirled round and round, catching his tail in his teeth and giving it a tug. He was so full of delight he didn't know what to do with himself.

At the last moment Frank reached for his mouth-organ where it had fallen amid the rockery. 'Mustn't leave this behind,' he said to Digby with a beaming smile. 'It brought us together again.'

Frank bought a food bowl and two tins of dog food. He sat on a bench and watched Digby devouring his meat. 'Now I'm really in a fix,' he thought, as the full force of his predicament struck him. 'It's Digby or the gardening job.' As he watched the collie enjoying his food, he noticed a little habit of Digby's that he thought he'd forgotten. Every time the dog caught Frank's eyes on him he gave a little answering wag of his tail before turning back to the bowl. This endearing characteristic was sufficient in itself to bring Frank to a decision.

'How could I do anything but keep you?' he said softly. 'I'm ashamed that I hesitated even for one second. We're a team, you and I, and we're going to beat the system. We need this job, both of us, and you're coming with me.'

Digby gave a little wag.

'Yes. I'll find a way. There's room for two in that little summerhouse and you'll have to learn to be as quiet as a little mouse.'

Digby wagged again.

'Tonight we'll sleep under the stars. And tomorrow you must spend one more day on your own. Miss Crisp is keeping your broken lead – I'm sure she'll be willing to keep you too.'

14

A final night under the railway arch passed without incident. Frank and Digby curled up together under the blankets, and at first light they went back to Keserly Street. Miss Crisp opened her door in her dressing-gown.

'Frank! What's this? Digby too! You found him! How wonderful.'

'He found me,' Frank explained. 'I don't know where he was taken or anything. But he's back, and that's all that matters.'

'Come in, do. I was just going to make some coffee. And Frank – I got your note. Thank you, but you didn't have to pay that money back. Really.'

'Yes, I did,' Frank insisted. 'It was a loan.'

'Well, tell me all about your new job. You wrote that it was gardening in a wilderness. Whatever did you mean?'

Frank described Rothesay House, the untended garden and the cabin.

'That's wonderful!' the kind woman cried. 'Everything's working out for you. *And* Digby. I'd given up hope, you know. Nobody seemed to know anything about him. My poster did no good at all.'

'Not quite everything's working out,' Frank said as he sipped his coffee. 'My new boss has banned the dog. He has one of his own.'

Miss Crisp was excited. 'But – what about Digby?' she stammered. 'You don't mean—'

'No, I don't mean you to take him,' Frank assured her. 'I'm going to smuggle him into my cabin. But I

can't do that until tonight. So just for today, could
you—'

'Of course!' she cried, muffling her disappointment.
'Though you could get into trouble, couldn't you? How
ever will you manage about feeding and exercising
him?'

'I'm not sure yet. No, I am about feeding. That's
easy. As for exercise – well, there's always night-time.'

'But the other dog?'

'That's my main worry. I'll have to be careful they
don't get introduced!' He laughed.

Miss Crisp shook her head. 'Doesn't seem feasible to
me. But it's your business, so I can only wish you the
best of luck.'

'I shall need it. Yet Mr Odling seems decent enough.
You never know; if I do all that's asked of me and make
a good job of it, he might change his mind.'

Coffee over, Frank prepared to leave, and Miss Crisp
had to get ready for work, too. Digby was shut in the
kitchen with some food and water. They closed their
ears to his objections.

'He can come out when I get home,' said Miss Crisp.
'What time will you be back?'

'As soon as I can after dark,' Frank replied. 'And
please – can I ask you not to risk letting him outside?
I don't want him bolting again. He'll have to hold on
somehow.'

At Rothesay House Mrs Odling answered the door. She
made Frank welcome and helped install him in the
cabin. He was still clutching the holdall and its con-
tents, which Miss Crisp had refused to take back.

'I think you've everything you need here,' Mrs
Odling said. 'There's bed linen and blankets in the
locker above the bed. I've bought you some tea and
coffee and bread to start you off. And a few tins of

odds and ends. If there's anything else you want, please ask.'

'I don't know what to say,' Frank murmured. He could hardly believe what was happening. He felt like a hotel guest, the comparison with his former existence was so marked.

Mrs Odling smiled. 'Then don't say anything,' she said kindly. 'My husband has told me what he wants you to do first. So, once you've sorted yourself out a bit, come round to the house. Mr Odling's at work now, so I'll show you where to begin.'

Frank could hardly bear to leave the cabin. He looked at everything over and over again, from the mats on the floor to the kettle to the bar of soap in the tiny bathroom, and had to keep reminding himself it was all for him. At length he realized he must look ready and eager to work, or it might be taken away again.

A surprise was waiting inside the house. Mrs Odling was in the kitchen with her dog, and Frank had to do a quick double take. The dog was a border collie just like Digby and for a fleeting second Frank thought Digby had somehow escaped and followed him. The likeness was uncanny. Mrs Odling noticed his preoccupation.

'Do you like border collies?'

'Oh yes. Very much. They're wonderful dogs.'

'Aren't they? This one's very friendly really, but he's a bit wary of strangers.'

Frank reacted suitably, his brain racing. Here was a bonus! If the family were fond of collies, maybe the objections to another one around the place would disappear. But he must be very cautious.

Mrs Odling took him to a particularly overgrown corner of the garden, where some azaleas were battling to bloom among a dense new growth of stinging nettles which threatened eventually to engulf them.

'This is the area my husband is most concerned about,' she said. 'The nettles are just dreadful. They'll choke everything if they aren't eliminated. I suppose you know all about weed and pest control, being a professional gardener?'

Frank gulped and nodded dumbly.

'Every preparation that can be sold must be in that shed over there,' Mrs Odling went on and laughed. 'You'll know what's best to use. We never got round to trying most of them.'

'Where do I put the rubbish?' Frank asked, hoping it was the right question. 'There will be a lot to dispose of.'

'That's a good point,' Mrs Odling admitted. 'I honestly don't know, Frank. Why don't you start your own compost heap in a suitable place? We're in your hands now.' She laughed again and left Frank to work things out for himself.

Inside the shed a multitude of boxes, jars and bottles met his eyes. He groaned. 'Where on earth do I begin?' he muttered. 'Ah well, I'll just have to read all the labels.' Besides the weedkillers, the shed contained a plethora of gardening tools. Frank selected what was most needed and drew on a pair of stout gardening gloves he found on a shelf. 'Here goes,' he told himself. 'I hope the lady's not watching.'

It was warm work but he quite enjoyed it once he got going. It was the sort of task you could undertake without having to think too much about it. So he thought about Digby instead and how, under cover of night, he was going to slip him into the cabin. Frank knew it was a betrayal of trust, but he reckoned that with the Odlings' good nature and love of dogs he could rely on Digby's own irresistible appeal to do the rest.

Taking no more than half an hour at midday to make himself a sandwich, Frank made great progress in his battle with the weeds. He wondered how long he was supposed to work, but since no one had said anything he simply stopped when he was tired. He sat in the cabin in the late afternoon, contemplating his new surroundings. There was a mass of work to be done, but it seemed he would be allowed to labour at his own pace. He knew very well Odling was taking full advantage of his vulnerability to underpay him. He began to wonder if the man knew something about his previous history of living rough. Why else had he suddenly appeared in the park to dangle the offer of a job with this unusual accommodation attached? But Frank didn't care. He stretched himself luxuriously in his chair and revelled in the unusual feeling of ownership.

When Odling returned home he came to inspect Frank's handiwork. He appeared pleased enough. 'You've made a reasonable start,' he said. 'Well done.'

Frank made himself a pot of tea and drank it slowly. He was itching for darkness to fall, but there were some hours of daylight left yet. He wondered if he had to ask permission to leave the premises but decided it was unlikely. When he thought it was time to go to Miss Crisp's, he left the cabin and locked the door. He loved the feeling of his own keys in his pocket. Odling was just leaving the house, and motioned to him.

'Are you going out?' he asked.

'Well, I was thinking of it, if that's all right?'

'Certainly. Would you be able to spare a few minutes to sort out some forms?'

'Of course. Shall I come now?'

'Thank you. Oh, look – you might find this useful. I notice you don't wear a watch.' Odling pulled a small alarm clock from his pocket. 'Would you like it?'

'I'd love it,' Frank answered. 'That's very kind.'

Half an hour later he was walking purposefully towards Keserly Street, anticipating Digby's welcome with excitement. On the way he bought some more dog food and biscuits, and a smart new lead. When he reached Miss Crisp's, she opened her door promptly.

'Everything's all right. He hasn't disgraced himself,' she announced.

'You've been wonderful,' Frank told her. Digby came bounding towards him, his tail thrashing to and fro, and leapt up with little whimpering cries of delight. 'I won't hang around,' Frank said. 'The poor dog must be desperate. Thank you again. I owe you so much.' He slipped the lead on to the blue collar and led the collie away, turning to wave at the corner. 'Miss Crisp's a real friend to both of us,' he told Digby. 'We must repay her kindness.'

Digby trotted along confidently. It had been awful spending so many hours alone in Miss Crisp's flat. All along, however, he knew Frank would return. The trust he had in his master was absolute.

They covered the distance to Rothesay House at a brisk pace. Luckily it was a dark night, thick clouds obscuring the stars. Frank's alarm clock showed it was nine thirty when they paused near the front gate. Frank made Digby sit, then he squatted down himself so that their eyes met.

'We have to be very quiet and very careful,' Frank whispered. 'Above all, *you* need to stay calm. Otherwise we might be in trouble.'

Digby licked his lips and tried to understand. He knew he was being cautioned. He felt Frank's hand smoothing his head and listened to his gentle voice repeating his command.

'Stay calm. Relax,' Frank was saying in a whisper. The words were soothing.

They entered the gate. Frank checked before moving any further. In the house the lights were on and the curtains drawn. The wild garden loomed black and almost impenetrable. Frank led Digby on tiptoe past the house, and then the wilderness screened them. They reached the cabin unchallenged. Frank unlocked the door and closed it noiselessly behind them.

'We're home, Digby.' He sighed with relief. 'Home. *Our* home.'

Digby wagged his tail happily, catching his young master's mood. Frank bent down to the lead. Digby was released and began to explore. Frank remembered to draw his own curtains before flicking on the light. 'Ah, this is marvellous,' he breathed, sinking into the only chair and leaning back, his hands behind his head. 'No more cold stones or squats for us.'

After Digby had been fed and watered Frank began to think about the next day. Their comfortable new life wouldn't be permanent unless they were very clever. In the early days of his employment it was essential for Frank to do nothing that would antagonize the Odlings. That meant that Digby must on no account be discovered. The cabin must be kept locked while Frank was working, just in case one of the family decided to visit it. As for the risk of Digby betraying himself by a bark or a whine – well, there was no sure way of preventing it. However, Frank thought that if he worked in an area close to the summerhouse for some days, it would help Digby to get used to his surroundings. The collie was more likely to be content in the knowledge that Frank was nearby, even if he didn't like being confined. But there was the problem of the nettles. Frank hadn't finished clearing them and the nettlebed was nowhere near the cabin.

'I'll have to go back to it later,' he decided. 'Can't have Digby wailing and whining with me out of sight.'

The next morning Frank looked for jobs close to home, and there were plenty of them. He was glad to see that the rhododendrons around the cabin made a good screen, and the windows revealed very little. As he started work, pruning and trimming, Frank kept an eye on the comings and goings of the family. Odling left for work first. Half an hour later the mother and daughter left the house. Frank guessed it was the school run. He dropped his tools and dashed to the cabin.

'Quickly now, Digby. We've a brief slot for you to get a breath of air and make yourself comfortable.'

They marched to the gate, Digby showing, unusually, a marked reluctance. He kept turning his head towards the house as though curious about what was in it, and only followed Frank in jerks and jolts. Frank kept a constant watch up and down the road as the collie took his hurried exercise. On the way back past the house Digby tried to dig his heels in again. Frank allowed him to pause for a few moments. Digby gave a strange sort of throaty growl and sniffed the air vigorously.

'Of course!' Frank cried. 'You can smell the other dog. I forgot that part of the puzzle! Now, suppose he smells you?'

There were no disturbances that day. Frank kept a careful note of Mrs Odling's absences. He meant to make himself familiar with the regular ones, such as delivering and fetching the daughter from school. That way he would get to know how long he had at his disposal to free Digby during daylight hours. In the evening, once everything was quiet, he took the dog for a long walk. It had rained again and now everything smelt fresh and scented under the trees lining the road. Frank thought a good deal about the Odlings' border collie. He guessed it was only a matter of time before the dogs would become fully aware of each other. The recognition would be bound to lead to a confrontation.

'So before that happens,' Frank thought, 'I need to make myself indispensable.'

15

During the next couple of days Frank worked with a will. Digby was getting used to the new routine and Frank felt free to return to the nettlebed. Odling only once came to speak to him, to ask how he was settling in. Mrs Odling allowed him to work without supervision or interference and merely gave him a smile or a wave when they glimpsed each other across the garden. Frank's compost heap was growing daily and, little by little, he was making an impression on the uncontrolled vegetation. Then came the weekend.

Frank intended to work all day on the Saturday. It was a fine sunny day and Frank was hoping the entire family would go out, taking their dog with them. He thought it would be nice for Digby to have the opportunity to join him in the garden for a while. However, time wore on and there was no movement from the house at all. Around eleven o'clock Frank decided to have a coffee break. He pacified Digby, who was disappointed that his master hadn't come back to the cabin to take him out.

'I know, I know,' he whispered to the dog. 'You must hang on somehow. We'll go the minute it's safe. I'm sorry. There, now. Have a biscuit. I'll be back just as soon as I can.' He sat on the grass in the sun with a mug of coffee. Presently he saw the Odlings' daughter approaching.

'Hello,' she said brightly. 'Aren't you doing well? Daddy's ever so pleased.'

Frank smiled. 'Is he now? I'm very glad.'

'Isn't it a lovely day?' The girl shaded her eyes from

the glare. 'Mummy asked if there's anything you need. I can fetch it for you if you like.'

'I don't think so,' Frank answered, 'nothing. Thank you. You're very kind. Er – are you going out today?'

'Oh, *I* don't know,' the girl said. 'They decide that. But I may have a friend round later.' She took a few steps towards the cabin. 'Is it comfortable in there?' she asked.

'Perfectly.' Frank watched her cautiously. 'It's a bit untidy, I'm afraid. You wouldn't want to see it.'

'Oh yes, I would,' she countered, laughing. 'I'd just love to see what you've made it look like. Men are so funny, aren't they? They seem to spread everything about all over the place. Daddy does, anyway.'

Frank quickly changed the subject. 'Don't you take your dog out?'

'Of course I do. We all take turns. And he's very interested in you. He's been really curious since you arrived. He spends a lot of time by the front door, sniffing and making little whiny noises. Perhaps if I let him out to see you properly he'd accept you better. Shall I fetch him?'

'No! I mean – er – not just now,' Frank replied awkwardly. 'I'm too busy.'

'You're not going to work today? It's Saturday!'

'I am – well, part of it, anyway.'

'Can I call you Frank?'

'Certainly you can. What do I call you?'

'My name's Harriet. Horrible, isn't it? But you can call me by my second name if you like. Everyone else does.'

'I think Harriet's a lovely name,' Frank said with a grin. '*I* shall call you that, if you'll let me?'

'Oh, all right then,' the girl said. 'I'm afraid I'd better go. I've got some homework to do and I want to get it out of the way early.'

She skipped away, leaving Frank to contemplate a narrow escape. He went back into the cabin, and Digby came begging to be taken out.

'I'm sorry, it's just no good at the moment,' Frank said. 'They're still around. We must try to be patient.'

He couldn't bear Digby's pleading looks and threw himself into some work. The nettles had almost been wiped out and he wanted to complete the job. At last there were some positive noises from Rothesay House. Mr Odling was backing his car from the garage. Frank stopped to watch. Then Mrs Odling and Harriet came out. The girl was holding the dog by the collar. The collie seemed to be searching for the source of a particularly interesting scent. Frank guessed what it was and could only watch helplessly. Suddenly the collie gave a little yap and broke free, making a beeline for Frank.

'He only wants to make friends,' Harriet called as Frank received the dog in a rush. The young man's clothes were of tremendous interest to the collie. Digby's scent was all over them and the collie wagged his tail and explored Frank's trousers and shoes as though desperate to find the answer to a longstanding puzzle. Frank tried to fend him off. He felt embarrassed by the dog's attention, with all the family looking on, and he wondered what it would lead to. Harriet ran over, laughing.

'He *does* seem to like you,' she joked. 'I told you he wanted to meet you!'

'Yes. He's very friendly, isn't he?' Frank said lamely.

'Come on, you silly creature,' Harriet said, dragging the dog away. 'You know Frank now. He's not so very different, is he?'

The collie was now pursuing the scent that had obsessed him since Frank's arrival, running his nose along the ground, pulling at Harriet's restraining arm.

He obviously wanted to go towards Frank's cabin, but the girl prevented him.

'No, no. Not now. We're going in the car,' Harriet told him.

Frank held his breath. He longed for the family to leave. He noticed Mr Odling was watching the dog with a puzzled expression.

'Hurry up, dear!' Mrs Odling called and Frank held himself rigid until everyone, dog included, was safely inside the car. Only when the Odlings had finally driven away was he able to relax.

'Phew!' He let out a long breath. 'That was too close for comfort. Now then, Digby, I think the rest of the day would be well spent away from here!'

Digby was only too happy to go anywhere that took him out of the cabin. Frank was amused to see he was eager to follow the other dog's scent, once he had picked it up on their way across the garden.

'Now you both know about each other,' Frank murmured. 'I wonder how long we'll be able to keep you apart?'

Frank decided to head for the park. It occurred to him that it was possible the Odlings might see him walking Digby from their car, so hurried him along to get away from the local streets. Once inside the park, Frank felt safe. Only a few days ago he had worked here. Now he was using the park for recreation like so many other people. He sat on a bench and let Digby roam around. For the first time since taking his new job Frank was able to play his mouth-organ. He hadn't dared to do so inside the cabin for fear of Digby's howls. Sure enough, the collie reacted.

'You're a soppy dog, Digby,' said Frank between tunes. 'You'll bring us an audience, but we don't need the money now.'

Some people were hovering nearby, showing the amusement the scene had always caused. Frank, intent on playing above the noise of Digby's howls, tried to ignore them. But when he stopped playing he nearly dropped his instrument. The Odling family were coming to see what all the fuss was about.

'Oh no!' Frank groaned. 'Why didn't I think of this?'

At the moment the family was on the other side of an expanse of grass, but their dog was off the lead and beginning to run. 'Digby, here! Quickly!' Frank leapt up and, with Digby at his heel, fled the spot. He had no idea if he had been recognized, but he cursed his own stupidity. The park, of course, was where James Odling had first encountered him. If he had thought about it, he would have realized it was a place the family was likely to visit at the weekend.

Frank and Digby hardly stopped running until they reached home. Frank bundled Digby out of sight and awaited the outcome. If they had been noticed, then the game was up. He knew Odling would be very angry about being tricked. It wasn't at all how Frank had planned things.

The family returned home around lunchtime and Frank expected Mr Odling to come marching up to the cabin straight away. But he didn't. An hour or so passed. Digby fell asleep on his blanket and Frank went cautiously outside. It was just possible that the little crowd which had gathered in the park as he played had obscured him sufficiently to escape recognition. He went back to his work. Shortly afterwards Odling came out.

'You're not obliged to work on Saturdays,' he said. 'I can't pay you any more.'

'That's all right,' said Frank with relief. 'I only wanted to get this bit finished.'

'You're very diligent. You've made a difference

already,' said Odling. 'I'm pleased with what you're doing. Do you need any money? I know it's not a full week yet, but you can have your wages early, if you like, and we can proceed from there and make each Saturday your payday.'

Frank took up the offer gladly. 'It would be very welcome,' he said. 'I do have quite a lot I want to buy.'

'I'll fetch the cash. You've still time to get to the shops. Er' – Odling jerked his head at the cabin – 'you managing all right? Everything working properly?'

'Perfectly, thank you, sir. I'm more than happy.'

'Good, good.' Odling went off for Frank's wages while Frank drew a deep breath. There was to be no investigation after all. But he must be much more careful. Perhaps he *should* only take Digby out at night.

Although they had escaped from the park, Frank and Digby were not entirely in the clear. The behaviour of the Odlings' dog was giving rise to some family curiosity. It appeared that all he wanted to do, as soon as Frank emerged each day, was to get out of the house. He begged to go out to him, wailing and barking alternately, until one of the family shut him away for the sake of peace. Harriet thought he should be indulged. At least if he were let outside, she reasoned, there was a chance he would satisfy himself about Frank and ultimately calm down. But, as they never gave in to him, the same scenes were repeated day after day. Harriet began to wonder just what was at the back of the collie's excitement. She made up her mind to try to find out.

One day after school she found Frank busy digging over a rosebed he had weeded. Harriet came out to him, carrying a glass of cold lemonade. 'Mummy thought you looked hot,' she explained.

'I *am* hot,' he said, taking the lemonade. 'Thanks. This is great.'

'Frank – did you ever own a dog?' Harriet asked abruptly.

Frank spluttered a little as he drank, taken aback. 'Um – yes,' he answered guardedly.

'What was it like?'

'Oh, you know, a mongrel,' he fibbed, thinking of Chip.

'It must have been fairly recently?'

'Not that long ago. Why?'

'Because our silly dog is going haywire since he smelt your dog on your clothes.'

Frank eyed the girl cautiously. How much did she know? Should he tell the truth and swear her to secrecy? He thought children loved to be trusted with a secret.

'I see,' he said. 'I – er – I'm sorry if it's causing trouble.'

'Not trouble exactly. But it's a nuisance. Dad is losing patience. We had another dog once but we had to get rid of him when we moved here. They were from the same litter. I never wanted them to be split up but Daddy insisted. He's not the greatest animal lover. What – what are you staring at?'

A light was beginning to dawn in Frank's mind. 'I'm sorry, I didn't mean to stare,' he said hoarsely. He gulped. 'What's your dog's name? No one's ever told me.'

'Tam.'

'Tam. And his brother was . . . ?'

'Digby.'

Frank sat down heavily by the rosebed. Here was a thing!

'Whatever's the matter?' Harriet asked. 'You look stunned.'

'That's just what I am,' Frank said. 'Look, Harriet, can I count on you as a friend?'

The girl was flattered. She smiled shyly. 'Of course you can.'

'I'm glad,' Frank said, 'because I'm in a spot of bother.'

Harriet drew herself up and tried to look very adult. 'Perhaps I can help?'

Frank smiled warmly, amused despite himself by her attitude. 'You can. I've something to tell you, but I must swear you to secrecy.'

Harriet's eyes popped. 'Yes? What's the secret?' she asked breathlessly.

'My dog wasn't a mongrel. He was – *is* – a border collie just like Tam. *Very* like Tam, in fact.'

Harriet gaped. 'You mean you have a dog *now*? Where is he?'

'In the cabin.'

The girl wanted to dash off at once to see him.

'Wait!' cried Frank, calling her back. 'Don't give the game away. I haven't told you all of it yet.' When he mentioned the Dogs' Home, Harriet began to shake her head slowly, anticipating the final revelation.

'It can't be,' she whispered. 'Not . . . not . . .'

'It's Digby,' Frank finished simply.

'Oh!' Harriet shrieked. 'Oh, *can't* I see him? It was so awful when we had to get rid of him – Tam and I missed him so. Oh, no *wonder* Tam's been acting the way he has. *Please* may I see him?' Her excitement faded a little. 'Oh – but what if Daddy finds out? He'll be so cross.'

'More than cross,' Frank said. 'I'll be dismissed.'

'But *why*?' Harriet sounded genuinely upset.

'He made it perfectly clear. No dogs.'

'You shouldn't have taken the job then,' Harriet said.

'That wasn't fair. Poor Digby. How could you keep him imprisoned in the shack like that?'

'He isn't imprisoned,' Frank assured her. 'Whenever the coast's clear I take him out. But it hasn't been easy. There's a lot I have to tell you about why I took the job and everything. I was desperate, you see, Harriet. I'd been living rough and your father's offer was just too good to resist. And Digby wasn't with me when I accepted it. I lost him for quite a while. Yes – it may have been wrong of me to smuggle Digby in. But for his sake as well as my own the thought of a bit of comfort and, above all, regular employment, was like a dream come true.'

Harriet nodded. She wondered if Frank was telling the truth. Snatches of plots from television dramas raced through her mind. 'You're not . . . on the run, are you?' she asked uncertainly.

Frank chuckled. 'No, I'm not on the run,' he replied. 'You've nothing to fear from me, Harriet. I'm not a criminal.'

'Oh, blow this "Harriet" business,' she cried. 'I'm only called that when I'm told off. Why don't you call me Millie like everyone else?'

'Millie. All right. If you prefer it? But I still like Harriet.' Frank looked toward the house. 'Are you expected back? I should tell you the whole story.'

Millie was eager to hear everything. 'I have to change,' she said. She was still in her school uniform. 'I'll come out later. And don't worry. I won't say a word.'

That night Millie lay in bed, her head still buzzing with all that Frank had told her. She longed to see Digby, but she and Frank had decided that that wasn't a good idea for the moment. Digby was sure to recognize her and where would that lead? She had promised Frank to act as a kind of sentry on his behalf; to give him a tip when she could as to when the family would all be out of the way, or to warn him to take extra care when her parents wanted to use the garden. But they both knew things couldn't continue as they were indefinitely. And what should they do about Tam?

'Digby and Tam should be together again,' Millie had said. 'I wish I could think of a way to talk Daddy round before he finds out our secret for himself.'

16

Digby found the regime at Rothesay House boring. He was left alone for long periods, and even when his master was with him he was always trying to quieten him down. Digby brightened up a bit when he detected signs of another dog in the vicinity, yet just when he wanted to investigate his master curtailed his activities even more. He caught the occasional sound of a bark from inside the house, but it was too muffled for him to interpret it. He thought about Streak a lot and wished he could be sure that the greyhound was safely back at home. Sometimes he thought about Chip, but he and Chip had never really been close companions by choice and the mongrel soon passed out of his mind again.

Meanwhile, inside Rothesay House, Tam was in a constant fever of impatience and exasperation. Ever since he had scented Digby on Frank's clothes he had known his brother must be nearby. Why was he, Tam, being prevented from finding him again? It was cruel. His owners were deaf to all his pleas to be released, but Tam could not stop begging, even though he knew his master's anger was just below the surface. Then one day it broke through.

'Whatever's wrong with the stupid dog?' James Odling cried sharply one evening. He had had a trying day and Tam's whimpers and wails were getting on his nerves more than usual. 'I'm fed up to the back teeth with his constant whingeing. Ever since Frank arrived he's been behaving like a mad creature. I'm going to get to the bottom of this!' He strode to the kitchen door where Tam was doing his best to get his nose through the crack underneath.

'Margaret!' he called to his wife. 'Look what this crazy animal has done to the bottom of the door. He's scraped every bit of paint off.' He yanked Tam away. 'Right, you barmy dog,' he snapped, 'if you want out you can have it.' He wrenched the door open, whereupon Tam dashed forth with all the pent-up energy of a caged beast.

He soon found the scent he had been so desperate to track. With mounting excitement, tail swinging, he set off towards the cabin. Odling went out to the garden. 'Going straight to Frank – I knew it,' he muttered, none too pleased. A couple of minutes later Tam began to bark. Digby's trail had ended at the cabin and his brother could not only smell him but hear him inside.

'Digby! Digby!' Tam called. 'It's me! Tam! Come outside, won't you? Let me see you.'

Frank had quickly muzzled Digby before he could respond to the barks outside. His hand gripped the collie's closed jaw and he clung on grimly, determined that no answering bark would give their secret away. 'It's all right, Digby,' he whispered. 'Keep calm. Don't vex yourself.' He struggled against Digby's efforts to get to the window. Tam continued to call. Frank knew the insistent barking would bring someone from the house. He hoped it would be Millie.

Suddenly the barking ceased. Pushing Digby behind him, Frank glanced out of the window. James Odling was by the door. He was holding Tam, who had instinctively quietened on the appearance of his master. Frank waited for the expected knock; the game was up.

'Frank, can I come in?' Odling called.

'Er – it's a bit messy in here, Mr Odling,' Frank replied. 'Shall I come out instead?'

'Just as you like.'

Frank cautioned Digby to be still and silent. Then he emerged from the cabin, quickly closing the door behind him and expecting any second the tell-tale sound from his collie which would bring their dismissal.

'I don't know what my dog finds so interesting in there,' Odling began. 'Can you throw any light on it?'

'No, Mr Odling. Perhaps it's the presence of somebody new in his garden that he objects to?'

'He doesn't object, does he?' Odling countered. 'Look at him! He's fascinated by you.' Tam was snuffling Frank's clothes with the greatest gusto.

Frank forced a laugh, not knowing what else to do. From the corner of his eye he spotted Millie coming to join them and hoped for a miracle. Tam started to paw and scratch at the cabin door.

'He just can't wait to see what's inside,' Odling went on. 'There's some mystery. Come on, Frank. You must know. What is it?'

Frank took a deep breath. It was no use. Millie could do nothing to prevent the inevitable. 'He can sense his brother's in there,' he explained, and immediately felt a tremendous relief.

'What? His brother? What are you talking about?'

'It's Digby,' Millie called as she came up. 'Frank has Digby in the shack, Digby's Frank's dog now.'

Odling's mouth dropped open and he gaped silently at his daughter. Then he pulled himself together. 'I don't know what's been going on behind my back,' he said angrily, 'but I want some explanations.'

Without a word Frank re-entered the cabin and led Digby outside. The two dogs jumped and leapt around each other uttering strange little cries of pleasure and recognition as they inspected one another with the

most searching sniffs. Odling watched in amazement
while Millie laughed joyfully and knelt to join in the
fun.

'This is quite incredible,' Odling said. He had forgotten momentarily, in his surprise, that Frank had
deceived him. 'Where did you find him?'

Frank explained, leaving nothing out, including the
bond he had felt between himself and Digby from
the very beginning.

'A strange story,' Odling commented, when he had
finished. 'But the fact remains, Frank, that I told you at
the outset there were to be no dogs. You've deliberately
flouted that condition. My requirement, however,
remains the same. We need a full-time gardener. We
don't need a second dog on the premises.'

Frank was silent.

'What shall it be, then?' Odling asked, ignoring
Millie who was trying to interrupt. 'You've settled in
well here. I'm quite happy for you to stay on, but Digby
must go. I took him to the Dogs' Home myself before
we moved here. I didn't expect to see him again and
this is all rather upsetting. But there must be many
other people willing to give him a good home.'

Millie was horrified. She looked from Frank's miserable face to her father's stern one. 'Daddy, you can't!
You can't make Frank do that,' she blurted out. 'He
loves Digby. Oh, Daddy, Digby's been no trouble, has
he? You didn't know he was here at all until just now.
You can't be so horrible!'

'It's all right, Millie,' Frank intervened before Odling
could reply. 'Your father's quite right. I've broken his
trust. I'm the one to blame, because I should never
have come here.' He looked at the other man. 'I'm
sorry for this upset, Mr Odling. I can't be parted from
Digby again. We'll go. I'll get my things together.'

'Oh no! No!' Millie protested in obvious distress.

'Don't let him, Daddy. Digby was ours once. Look at Tam. He's overjoyed.'

'You needn't go straight away,' James Odling said hurriedly. 'You can stay on here until you've found somewhere else. I mean,' he added awkwardly, realizing the only other option for Frank was to return to living rough, 'a – a flat or something. I wouldn't want you to be forced back on to the streets because of me. If you prefer to find another job where you can keep Digby, that's fine by me. Whatever you think best.' He put his arm round his daughter. 'I'm sorry, Millie. But you must remember how it was before with the two dogs. It was just too much. I'll do what I can to help Frank, I promise.'

Millie took heart. Frank and Digby were not to be banished immediately. She had time to get to work on her father, who might be persuaded over the next day or two, especially if she enlisted her mother's help. And her mother still didn't know about Digby. 'I must tell Mummy!' she said, and ran off.

The two men looked at each other unhappily. 'I'm sorry, Frank,' said Odling.

'Don't be,' Frank answered. 'I'm sorry I tricked you.'

Odling shrugged. He caught hold of Tam's collar and separated the collies. Frank saw the simple action as symbolic. Odling and Tam went back into the house, and Frank sighed. He knew he would have to put Digby back in the Dogs' Home. Frank couldn't provide him with a proper home and he owed it to Digby to give him a better chance next time round than he had brought him.

For the rest of the evening Frank sat in the cabin that was no longer his and brooded. He had no intention of staying on as gardener when he had taken Digby back to the Dogs' Home. He felt it would be a kind of treachery. Besides, seeing Tam day after day would be a constant reminder of his banished pet. He didn't know where he could go from here. But go he would – and soon.

The next day Millie brought Tam into the garden as soon as she got home from school. Frank had finished off a job in the garden which he didn't want to leave half done and was in the middle of collecting his few clothes and belongings together. He meant to leave by stealth at night without a further word. He closed the cabin door as he saw Millie approaching and went to meet her. She was smiling broadly.

'It'll be all right, Frank, I know it will,' she said. 'Daddy's not made of stone and I've got Mummy on my side already.'

Frank refrained from comment. He fetched Digby and he and Millie watched the two dogs waltzing around each other like two puppies, uttering their little cries of delight.

'They're talking to each other,' Millie cried.

Frank managed a half-hearted laugh. 'Well, they have a lot to tell one another,' he said.

It was a warm, sunny evening. The dogs chased up and down, gambolling across the lawn and crashing in and out of the undergrowth until they were tired out. Then they lay down together, side by side, their tongues lolling, in a patch of shade under the rhododendrons.

'Life has been so dull since you left.' Tam told his brother. 'This is more than I ever hoped for. I couldn't understand what happened to you. That awful day when the master came back without you!'

'Awful,' Digby repeated, and shuddered. 'I was lucky to have a friend in the compound who managed to keep me calm.'

'You always had a jangly tendency,' Tam chided him affectionately.

'It's been my undoing, hasn't it? But here we are together again. It's so wonderful. I still can't believe it.'

'Oh, I scented you as soon as I got close to your master,' cried Tam. 'I couldn't get to you. It was so infuriating. I made their lives a misery, I think, with my complaints.'

'Well, that's nothing. I've had my share of suffering,' Digby told his brother. 'Wait till you hear what I've been through.'

'Tell me, tell me,' begged Tam. 'I want to know everything.'

'You shall. But not now. Don't let's spoil the moment. We have plenty of time. And they're coming to fetch us again.'

17

As soon as it was quite quiet in the house, Frank led
Digby into the dark garden. In his left hand he carried
the holdall with everything he owned in it. Minutes
later they were on the road to the railway arch. Frank
left no note of explanation. He knew Millie would be
upset by his departure and he was sorry for it. But now
he could think only of the awful separation to come.

Digby trotted along happily, enjoying the night air.
He believed he was simply out for a walk. When they
reached the railway arch and Frank began to bed down,
Digby was ready for a night under the stars. He would
have been content to spend every night in this way so
long as Frank was with him. For, marvellous as it was to
be reunited with Tam, Digby would leave him without
hesitation if Frank demanded it. The two companions
fell asleep, wrapped up together in a rough blanket.

The dread morning arrived, and they were on their
way again at an early hour. Digby was puzzled as he
recognized the route to the compound, and began to
pull on the lead. He wanted to get past the spot quickly.
Frank mistook his anxiety for a surprising eagerness to
reach the Dogs' Home itself, and was taken aback. Had
Digby really been happier there than with him? It was
a chastening thought. Frank was more depressed than
ever.

They approached the entrance, and Digby pulled
harder still. As they stopped by the outer door the
collie suddenly sensed that something was wrong, and
when they went through the door and into the yard he

started to panic. The smells were horribly familiar. Frank tried in vain to calm him. By the time they were inside reception, Digby was beside himself. Frank felt nothing but loathing for his own actions, yet he was convinced there was no alternative. He simply wanted to get the awful admission procedures over as quickly as he could and get out of there.

While the business was done he was in a daze, conscious only of Digby's fright. When Digby had been led away and Frank was outside in the street again, he had no idea what to do, nor where to go. He felt utterly friendless. It seemed to him that this betrayal – the betrayal of Digby's loyalty and love – was the worst thing he had ever done. And it was no solace to think that Digby would in the end live a happier and more comfortable life. Frank felt a new and terrible loneliness, which blocked out all other feelings.

Frank's disappearance wasn't noticed at Rothesay House until late afternoon. Mrs Odling told Millie on her return from school that he hadn't been seen all day, and she had assumed he had gone looking for other employment. Millie was at once suspicious.

'Is he there now? Have you been to look?' she demanded. She rushed into the garden with Tam who, of course, ran straight to the cabin. Millie's cries brought her mother running.

'He's gone! Digby's gone!' the girl was wailing. 'Look – the key's in the door. Frank's taken all his things and left! Oh – why did Daddy have to drive him out?'

'He didn't drive him out,' Mrs Odling corrected her at once, 'and you know it. Daddy was quite fair about it. There was no need for Frank to leave like this without a word. Whatever possessed him?'

'He's gone,' Millie repeated tearfully. 'He won't be back. Don't you see?' She was devastated. Her plan to persuade her father that Digby should stay for Tam's sake was in ruins. She hadn't even begun to try.

'He's a very silly young man,' Mrs Odling was saying. 'We owe him almost a week's wages. I can't believe he won't come back for that. He must need it.'

'He won't, he won't come back,' Millie sobbed. 'I know he won't. And we'll never be able to find him again.'

Inside the Dogs' Home the afternoon sun shone into Digby's pen. Digby lay on the concrete floor, trembling visibly. His misery was total. He had been abandoned again, and this time by the person he trusted above all others. A bowl of food lay untouched to one side. Number One was yelling for attention, just as he always did when the visitors arrived. Digby raised his head slightly. He felt a pang of regret for Number One, who apparently had no hope of ever being selected. That brought him back to the realization that somebody else would in all likelihood select himself, as they had before. Digby couldn't bear the thought of more strangers, more unhappiness . . . and for what? So that, after a short period of time, he would find himself back here again? He sighed deeply and rested his head on his paws.

Then something made him sharply alert again. Among the medley of barks objecting to Number One's endless boasts was one well-remembered voice. Chip! Digby perked up just a little. There was no Streak in the neighbouring pen to cheer him up but, listening to Chip's remonstrances, Digby didn't feel quite so alone.

'Take me! Take me!' Number One bellowed hopelessly.

'I wish somebody *would* take you,' Chip was yapping. 'Give us a break from the monotony.'

'Chip!' Digby called. 'Can you hear me? It's Digby! Where are you?'

Eventually the barking died down a little. Digby renewed his calls and Chip heard him.

'I'm not so far away, I think. You sound close,' the mongrel called. 'How did you end up in here?' The voice seemed to come from across the passage.

Digby got up and went to peer through his grille. To his surprise and pleasure he could see Chip standing with his nose to his own grille a couple of pens along on the opposite row. Their tails wagged briefly as they spotted each other.

'I've been abandoned again,' Digby informed Chip sadly.

'So I see.'

'What about you, Chip?'

'Oh, I've been here quite a while. I told you: I'm a regular Jack-in-the-box, I am. In and out of here like . . . but wait a moment! You said "abandoned". Last time I saw you, you were with another man in a car. You know – after you were captured and tied up.'

'That's right. I've had some narrow escapes. I found my master again, but it was all in vain. Look at me now.'

'Don't feel so sorry for yourself,' Chip barked. 'You'll soon be picked out again. Just think of that poor brute Number One! He's the sort we should be sorry for.'

Digby knew the remark was justified but it didn't lift his spirits. He began to tell Chip all about his adventures. Then the visitors reached their row and occupied their attention. Digby made himself as unappealing as he was able by growling and baring his teeth at all of them.

Later he continued his talk with Chip, and learned that Streak had been briefly in the Dogs' Home again. Digby guessed the greyhound had lost his way running from the hateful Ken. However, his owners had claimed him shortly after his arrival in the compound.

'Oh, that's good news,' Digby said, forgetting his own troubles for a moment. 'I wondered about him. Bouncing Jet Streak of Fleetwood,' he recited affectionately. 'A true friend.'

'Oh yeah? I could do with one or two of those,' Chip muttered a mite enviously.

'Well, I . . . we can talk together, can't we?' Digby offered.

'Yeah. We can. Thanks, Digby.'

Chip's presence did help. The two dogs communicated when they could. At night, though, Digby's spirits sank. In the darkness, when most of the animals were asleep, he would think about Frank and Tam until, released from sorrow by sleep, he dreamed of them instead.

But there was a further blow to come, and a most unexpected one. Norman, now fully recovered, had resumed his way of life as a pub singer. One of the managers he knew well had given him a room above the pub, and one afternoon, having already combed the streets and drawn a blank, he arrived at the Dogs' Home, looking for Chip.

The old man wasn't particularly fond of dogs in general and he paid scant attention to most of them. He came heavily along the corridor, humming an air, and let out a piercing whistle when he spotted Chip.

'Bless my soul, here you are then!' he cried delightedly. 'This is magic for both of us. Oh, you're glad to see me, are you?' Chip was yelping in greeting, and Norman bent down and tickled the mongrel's ears. 'Wait on a bit. I'll have you out in no time.' Pleased as Punch at finding his old comrade again, Norman set off to make arrangements.

When Chip was removed from his pen, Digby whined

miserably as the mongrel gave him a cheery last call. 'I'll see you outside, Digby. I'll look for you!'

Digby was too upset to respond. Now his last friend was taken from him. Frank, Tam, Streak and, finally, Chip: all gone, all distant. He lay with his head on his paws, his misery complete.

At Rothesay House, too, unhappiness prevailed. Ever since Frank and Digby's departure, Millie had been sullen and unforgiving. She held both her parents to blame. Her father had presented Frank with an impossible ultimatum, and her mother, Millie thought, had been uncaring. Moreover, Tam had begun to fret. He was off his food, listless and withdrawn. Mr Odling despaired.

'We don't owe them anything, Margaret,' he said, trying to justify himself. 'The lad was only a gardener, after all. The business of Digby is unfortunate and I suppose, with hindsight, I was a bit peremptory, but . . . well, all this' – he waved an arm at his daughter, sulking in a chair – 'is just ridiculous.'

'You *do* owe Frank,' Millie contradicted. 'His wages!'

'It's not my fault he went off without them,' Odling protested.

'Of course not, dear,' his wife agreed. 'But, James – don't you think we should make some effort to locate Frank? I'm really worried about him. He has no home, you know.'

Odling looked shamefaced. 'I know,' he mumbled. 'But I couldn't have foreseen his moonlight flit. I never dreamed he would do such a thing. I thought he'd at least stay on until he could sort himself out.'

'What about Tam?' Millie demanded. 'Why should he go on suffering?'

There was silence. There was no doubt Tam was very unhappy.

James Odling heaved a deep sigh. 'All right,' he said at last. 'I can't stand this atmosphere any longer. How can we find Frank?'

'Why don't we try the park?' Margaret Odling suggested. 'That's where you found him first. Tomorrow's Saturday, so we could all go.'

Millie wasn't convinced. 'What would Frank be doing in the park, Mummy? He doesn't have a job there any more.'

'Can you think of anything better?' James Odling asked irritably.

Millie looked at Tam lying under a chair, head on paws in an unconscious reflection of Digby. 'Actually I can,' she said. 'Why not let Tam look for Digby? The first thing he does when he gets outside is to sniff Digby's scent. Why don't we let him lead us?'

'Millie, he's not a bloodhound. He's a collie,' Margaret Odling pointed out.

'He's more likely to know where to go than we are, anyway,' Millie insisted stubbornly. 'We could at least try.'

'Yes,' her father said. 'We could. We'll give it a go, Millie.'

18

The next day Tam was put to the test. He was so eager to find his brother again that, once on Digby's trail, he pulled like mad on the lead to follow it. Millie's arm was stretched to the limit but she didn't complain or haul the dog back. Her parents walked behind, resigned but curious.

Tam, as the family soon discovered, wasn't the greatest canine sleuth. He lost Digby's scent early on, then found it again by a lamp-post farther down the street and showed tremendous excitement. From there he managed to track his brother to the railway arch where Frank and Digby had sheltered. The scent was so strong thereabouts that Tam spent some minutes casting about, in and out of the arch and round the corner, this way and that, until Millie tired and pulled him up.

'He's not here any more, Tam,' she told the collie. 'Can't you find which way he went?'

Her parents had watched Tam's antics. 'He's stumped,' James Odling said. 'Come on, Millie. It's no use. We can't stay here.'

Margaret Odling had a thought. 'This isn't far from the Dogs' Home where you first took Digby,' she said. 'Do you think Frank might have taken him back there? After all, he'd have difficulty looking after him without a job, or a roof over his head.'

Millie glared at her father, and Odling raised his eyes to heaven.

'All right, all right. I'm the villain of the piece. I know.' He hated to see his daughter's accusing looks.

'Let's go to the Dogs' Home, and if Digby's not there we'll simply have to give up. What more can we do?'

In the compound, Millie was saddened by the collection of abandoned, lost and stray dogs. Her soft heart melted when she saw the animals' puzzled or downcast expressions. Even those who perked up at the sight of the interested and sympathetic human onlookers were, she knew, doomed to disappointment as the family eventually passed them by.

'How could you, Daddy? How could you have brought poor Digby to this kind of place?' she whispered.

'Stop blaming your father,' Margaret Odling said a little sharply. 'He's not a criminal. You don't understand. There are times when unpleasant things have to be done. And he's doing his best to make up for it now.'

'I'm sorry, Daddy,' Millie said. Then, suddenly, 'Look! Look at Tam!'

Tam was lunging forward, trying to break into a run. Millie let him have his head. The two scampered down the corridor and Tam's explosive yelps of delight and excitement brought the adults hurrying up. And there were the brother collies, one outside the pen doing his best to get in, the other behind the grille scrabbling to get out; both straining to cross the barrier between them.

'Oh, look. Look at them!' Millie laughed joyfully. 'They're so pleased to see one another!'

Even her father had to admit that the dogs obviously belonged together. 'Very well. We must go to the office and explain everything,' he said. 'I hope they won't make any objections. I don't expect they'll remember me, but if they do I'll make them understand I made an awful mistake.'

Millie was ecstatic. But there was still the question of Frank's whereabouts.

Frank had skulked from street to street, using up what money he had on food and sleeping wherever the mood took him. After a few days he realized he needed to stop drifting. Digby was in the Dogs' Home, so the job at Rothesay House could yet be his. It was a tempting thought for someone who had recently got used to feeling comfortable, but it was a thought Frank dismissed almost as soon as it took shape. He had betrayed Digby's trust once. To return to Rothesay House without him would be a double betrayal. He wondered if anyone had chosen Digby and taken him home. If so, he hoped it was to a more settled existence than he had provided. He still regretted the number of hours Digby had had to spend shut away in the cabin.

The more Frank thought about Digby's prospects the more he longed to know his fate. Although he wanted the best for Digby, he was unable to prevent himself from wishing the collie was still in the compound. Somehow it felt that while Digby was being housed by the charity in the Dogs' Home, he was still Frank's dog. Finally, Frank resolved to return there. He simply had to know what had happened.

On the way he began to make all kinds of plans. He decided that if he found Digby still penned up, he would see it as Fate taking charge. It would then be Frank's duty to spare his dog any more unhappiness. Somehow he would arrange to get him out. Then the two of them could resume their old life as it had been before the Odlings had come into it. Digby had been content then; he could be so again. Frank grew more and more excited as he neared the building. As he entered it, he felt as though a weight had dropped

from his shoulders. He smiled at everyone he saw as
he began the familiar route around the corridors and
then up the ramps to the higher levels. The smile faded
as he reached the top floor without finding any sign of
Digby.

'He *must* be here. He *must*,' he muttered fiercely to
himself, his eyes scanning the name plates outside the
few empty pens in case Digby had been temporarily
removed for exercise or medical attention. But his
name appeared nowhere. Frank realized the worst had
happened. Digby had been readopted.

As a last resort he went down to the office to enquire
about the date of Digby's selection. The young girl on
duty recognized him.

'Have you had a change of heart?' she asked.

'No. Well – yes,' Frank answered uncertainly. 'When
did Digby go? Were they nice people? Did he look
happy?'

The girl smiled. 'They were very nice people. They
came only yesterday. And – er – is your name Frank?'

'Yes. Yes, it is. Why?'

'I have a message for you. From the little daughter.
She said we were to tell you, if you ever came here
looking, that Digby is safe and well and will be longing
to see you.'

'But – but . . .' Frank's mind raced. 'Was the little
girl called Millie?'

'That's right.'

'Oh!' Frank cried. 'Now I see! That's great! So they
changed their minds too. Digby is back with his
brother.'

'He was here,' the girl confirmed. 'He came with the
family. He and Digby looked like two peas in a pod.'

'Of course. They're from the same litter. Thank you
so much; you've made my day.' Frank sighed happily.
'Oh, this is more than I hoped for. I must go and see

poor Digby. He can't know what's happening to him. He's been in and out of one place and another . . .' Frank's voice died away as he strode to the exit. He was talking to himself more than to anyone else.

After a hasty clean-up, he set off for Rothesay House. His head was in a whirl. What had changed Odling's mind? 'It's Millie. I bet it's Millie,' he murmured to himself. 'I'm so glad Tam and Digby are together. But what about the garden? Is someone else looking after that? And if not, can I have my job back? But if I do, who does Digby belong to? He's not mine any more. I gave him up. Oh! Oh dear! But at least I'd see him . . .'

On and on went Frank's thoughts. They couldn't be put to rest until he arrived at the house. It was Sunday, the weather was fine and the family were all in the garden, eating a cold lunch. Millie heard the doorbell ring. She came running when she saw who it was.

'Frank! Oh, Frank!' She flung her arms round him in a joyful hug. 'Mummy! Daddy! It's Frank!' She grabbed Frank's free hand and dragged him after her.

Millie's parents stood up to greet him. Both had relieved smiles on their faces. Before anyone could speak Digby bounded from cover and leapt into Frank's arms, plastering his face with frantic licks.

'Well!' James Odling laughed. 'That says it all, Frank. Welcome back. We've made mistakes, both of us. The garden has missed you, as you can see. And – and so have we,' he ended a little awkwardly.

Frank couldn't find words. He stood smiling broadly, but with a slightly dazed expression.

'The cabin's yours as before,' Margaret Odling said, 'unless' – she looked momentarily uncertain – 'you've found another position?'

'Er – no. No, nothing,' Frank stammered, stooping to drop Digby to the ground. He hardly dared ask about the dog. 'Er – can Digby . . .'

'Digby will want to be with you,' Margaret Odling said. 'I think he's made that quite plain.' She laughed. 'And perhaps with Tam too!'

The other collie was standing nearby, enjoying the scene and wagging his tail sympathetically.

'Thank you,' Frank said. 'But I think Digby belongs to all of us.'

Some days later Frank sat in his cabin with the door open on to the garden. He had invited Miss Crisp to tea. They watched the two dogs lying peacefully side by side in the shade of the rhododendrons. Occasionally one would utter a contented sigh which the other would echo.

'You haven't told me your story yet,' Tam reminded Digby.

'Plenty of time for that,' Digby said. 'I'm savouring every moment as it passes. It's so wonderful to feel settled when you've lived through something so different.'

'Well, that's what we are,' said Tam. 'Settled for life.'